BEFORE THE FLOOD

BOOK I – THE AWAKENING

By

Balewa Sample

Before the Flood I. The Awakening by Balewa Sample

Cover Design: Rebecacover

Editor: Art Fogartie

Prologue

There was time when the Earth was young – much younger than today – when the air was pure and the animals docile – when Humanity and Nature lived in cooperation instead of competition.

There was time when simple folk attached magical powers – even divinity – to anyone they encountered whose abilities, strength, agility, or prowess exceeded their own.

There was a time when our planet was the target of exploration just as, eons later, the Americas lured men to board ships and sail to the edge of the world.

There was a time when "story" meant more than "data" – when complex circumstances found clarification in simple stories – when the most logical explanation of life, death, fortune, victory, defeat, love, success, and failure was always the same sentence: *It is the will of the gods.*

There was a time...

Foreword

Long, long ago when the Earth was young...

In the eastern central section of Pangea (the area now known as Africa) stood the kingdom of Abzu – the Land of the People with Elongated Skulls. Though not the largest by area, it was the most powerful. Its resources dwarfed those of other city-states, its pitch-black soil never failed to produce bountiful harvests. The Abzubian plains featured the freshest, emerald green grass ever seen and crystal-clear water filled the citizens' cisterns and wells.

Gigantic zebras roamed the pampas. Prides of lions dotted the rolling hills. The only fish in the rivers larger than the plump stumpnose, musselcracker, and grinders were the salmon, which routinely exceeded the size of a small child. No one lived in fear of the beasts, for legend said the great god Shango had taught the inhabitants the ability to train the beasts that could be domesticated and to hunt the ones that could not be tamed.

The air virtually sparkled with cleanliness and the bounty of minerals from the hills equaled or exceeded the plentiful nature of the fields. It was paradise.

The people lived in pyramid-like shelters impervious to the elements. Pleasant, cool nights routinely followed balmy, tropical days. The abundance of floral made the area oxygen rich, which in turn caused the plants and flowers to flourish all the more and live longer.

Life was good – life was pleasant – life was safe.

And the great god Shango presided over it all.

CHAPTER 1

A long time ago...

"Are the gods angry, Grandfather?"

"No, Omari. They just like to demonstrate their power from time to time."

The old man looked down at his grandson. At four and a quarter cubits[1], Dindaka had been the tallest man in the Kingdom in his prime. Years of labor and the weight of leadership now bowed his back. His snow-white hair pointed more towards the landscape than towards the sky and every day his hunched shoulders seemed to stoop more. But his physical infirmity had not diminished his intellect, his authority, or his status in the tribe. His wisdom was unassailable.

"They are preparing for battle, but it is not a real contest," Dindaka said. "I have seen this many times before."

The citizens of Abzu riveted their expectant eyes on the head of the Dogon Tribe – the leaders of the nation as long as anyone could remember. In his time, Dindaka had seen more sunsets...tracked more game...and killed more enemies than anyone in the Kingdom.

Young Omari continued asking questions, as always. "Will there be a storm, Grandfather?"

Dindaka extended a gnarled hand and patted his grandson on the head.

"No, Omari," he said. "But when Shango and Ogun collide, it will seem like one."

The youngster's eyes burned with inquisitive fire.

"Why will they do this, Grandfather?"

A slight smile cracked the edges of Dindaka's mouth. "Why do men ever fight?" he asked.

Omari knew a test when he heard one. He stood erect, forefinger to his lips in thought. "There are three reasons, Grandfather," he said reciting one of the lessons he'd learned at the old man's knee.

"And they are?"

"Land."

A nod.

"Pride."

Another nod.

The boy hesitated.

"Go on, boy," Dindaka said. "You are allowed to recite your lessons."

"S...s...sex," the boy said. "The last reason is almost always a woman."

Dindaka's head bobbed. "The last reason, which is almost always the first reason," he said. "Someone has a woman that someone else desires."

Omari shook his head. "I understand the first two reasons, Grandfather," he said. "But why would anyone ever fight because of a girl ?– especially brothers. Seems like a silly reason."

Dindaka laughed aloud at this grandson's sincerity. "You are correct, Omari," he said. "It is a silly reason. But you will understand it very clearly when you get older."

A scowl slid across the youngster's face. "You always say that, Grandfather, especially when we talk about women. How long before I understand ?"

Dindaka took stock of the lad, his long legs, his gangly arms, the wisps of hair on his chin.

"Sooner than you think, grandson. Sooner than you think."

**

Shango stood, hands on hips and laughed.

"That is the dumbest looking helmet I have ever seen, brother," he said.

Ogun did not return the smile. His obsidian eyes flashed from behind a bronze faceplate. "To be a god, dress like a god," he said.

"Don't you think the feathers are a bit much?"

Ogun raised a massive hand and stroked the lavender plumage sprouting from the top of his helmet. "When I am standing over you in victory, you can laugh, brother. Until then, show some respect for your elders."

Shango laughed – an echoing chortle that cascaded down the mountain to the crowds below. The natives could not understand the conversation – it was in the foreign tongue known only to the gods – but they could see the two massive bodies on the

9

slope above, and they could hear the laughter. It sounded malevolent and – god-like.

Although only the oldest and wisest like Dindaka knew it (and were prohibited from discussing it) the impending battle was a sham, a game Shango and his older brother had been planning for a while. Neither was contesting hunting or real estate rights, and both had all the women they wanted. But each man was fiercely prideful. Their playful sibling rivalry always began in jest – and almost always ended with someone's face bloody.

As they headed to the Field of Conquest high above the village of Blandika, Ogun turned to Shango, "Let's put on a show for your beloved human beings."

Shango looked over his shoulder. "I am not their creator," he said.

"But you are the God of Thunder," Ogun said. "You bring the rain."

Shango roared another laugh. "It rains when it rains, dear brother. You and I both know I have nothing to do with it."

The brothers stood on the high plateau, one hundred and fifty feet above the collected citizens who gaped first, then bowed in awe. Resplendent in their armor, Shango and Ogun faced off, then took flight.

The battle was fierce or so it seemed to those watching. The two huge deities (both over five cubits[2] tall) crashed into each other with mountain-shaking force.

When the ground trembled after one, particularly violent collision, Omari clutched his grandfather's hand. "Will the mountain collapse?" he asked.

"Not until the gods wish it to fall," the old man said.

The spectacle went well. Neither brother's body or ego suffered. After twenty minutes, Shango stood over his vanquished brother who was too weak – or so it seemed – to stand after slamming into a boulder. Ogun held up his hand. In a loud voice, he said, "I yield to the God of Thunder."

A chant swelled from the assembled. "Praise be to Shango. Praise be to the God of Thunder."

The people knelt and prayed, thanking the Father God for his benevolent and all-power son. Shango extended his hand and helped an over-acting Ogun to his feet.

"Careful, brother," Shango said. "They will spot a farce if you play this like one."

Ogun sneered. "They are sheep. They will believe what we want them to believe."

Arms over one another's shoulders, the brothers each raised a clenched fist in triumph as they disappeared into the Cave of Mystery. A thick, gray cloud appeared and blocked the entrance from view.

On the other side of the door, both brothers unbuckled their belts, then collapsed.

"You hit me a little hard with that thunder

clap," Ogun said. "My ears will be ringing the rest of the day."

Shango pointed an accusing finger. "Just a little something I designed, Ogun," he said. "I was only following your lead. The boulder to the back of my head was not in the script, dear brother."

"Just a little improvisation to keep it interesting." Ogun massaged his tender chest before continuing. "Did you see their faces?" Ogun asked. "They fear us."

"Yes," Shango said. "They believe we control all things."

"And they never stop asking. More food... more rain...more bounty. When will they get enough?"

"They give us what we need."

Ogun leered. "And what we want, lord brother."

"The women they send to us are more that willing," Shango said. "But they are mere distractions."

"They help us pass the time while we are here," Ogun said.

"And we should not care about anything else," Shango said. "We have work to do here."

"And we have been here a very long time," Ogun said. "So, we might as well enjoy it a little."

"You make a valid point, Ogun, my brother. Just remember, as long as they mine the gold and offer it every week, what do we care. The meager gifts we give them cost us nothing. We take the crops from one tribe and give them to another. "

Ogun mounted the steps to his silver dragon, the one that would return him to his kingdom. He turned to Shango and spoke. "Which reminds me. When we fight tomorrow before the Eleeka Tribe, it's my turn to win."

Shango smiled. "I never forget, brother," he said. "You never let me forget."
**

The young girl watched from the valley. Where some saw arrogance, she imagined confidence. What some described as self-promotion, she believed to be leadership. When others cowered in fear, she wanted to be noticed.

She looked at her companion, Naomi, and said, "I think he is wonderful."

Naomi patted her hand and said, "He does not know you are alive."

The young girl stretched her long neck. "It does not matter. Eventually, he will know who I am. I will be all he thinks about."

"Whatever you want to believe," Naomi said, laughing.

Once more, the young girl looked stared up toward the bluff where the battle had taken place. Once more, Nefertari, ten-year-old sister of King Gamba thought of Shango – and fell in love.
**

"How do they fly, Grandfather?" Omari stared at the vacated plateau in wonderment.

"They are the gods," Dindaka said. "They are

too powerful for the Mother."

"The Mother?"

"You must pay more attention to your studies, Grandson," the old man said sternly. "One day, you will be called on to instruct – perhaps to lead. You must have knowledge."

"I know, Grandfather," the boy said. "I am sorry, but school is boring; there are so many more interesting things to do."

Dindaka nodded. "I know," he said. "I was young once." He stared at the sky.

"Grandfather?"

"Yes, boy?"

"The Mother? You were going to tell me..."

"Oh yes, the Mother – the Mother of us all – the Mother of the Earth, loving and tender. Without her care, we would be flung into the Dark Sea of Nothingness, but she holds us to her body. She keeps us close."

"How?"

"The Mother has countless arms and hands. They are strong, but not as powerful as the gods. We cannot see the Mother's appendages, but we can smell them in the freshness of a dewy morning or the fragrance of the honeysuckle. She has you now, boy, holding onto you tenderly lest you slip into the abyss."

Omari shuddered.

"I sure hope she pays better attention to me than I do in school."

Dindaka patted the boy on the head. "Be sure

of it," he said. "Be absolutely sure of it."

CHAPTER 2

Six years later...

Shango stared so hard at the young woman on the other side of the room that he missed his mouth with the wine goblet. The deep burgundy liquid slid across his chin and down his shirt.

Still, he stared.

Ogun noticed. "See something you like, dear brother?"

Shango nodded, unable to speak.

Ogun decided to have some fun. "Notice how her legs flow like water. She moves with the grace of an antelope in full gallop. She is shapely and lithe all at the same time. I imagine she could kill a man during passion."

Shango gulped audibly.

"I...I...I have never seen such a creature," he said.

"She is no different from any of the other hundreds of women you have had, brother," Ogun said. "And, guessing her age, I would imagine she lack certain skills you would require."

Shango kept staring. His only response was, "Uh huh."

Ogun's brow furrowed. "Seriously, brother, she is a baby. What about her is so special?"

"I do not know," Shango said. "But I have never felt this way before in my life."

Ogun motioned to a servant. The man hustled to the table.

"Bring that young woman over here," he said.

"If she wishes, Lord Ogun," the servant said.

Before the God of War could question the response, the servant slid across the room, and approached the young woman. He whispered into her ear. She turned, looked at the head table, laughed, and resumed her animated conversation.

The servant approached Ogun with his head bowed.

"The lady refuses your invitation, my Lord," he said.

"It was not an invitation," Ogun said. "It was a summons."

He began to rise, but Shango's hand held him in place. "If the lady refuses to come to see us, brother, I will go to see the lady."

Shango stood and walked across the crowded hall. Everyone tried to act disinterested, but every eye furtively watched as the scene unfolded. The great god Shango rarely left his seat during a feast unless it was to indulge in a sexual dalliance with a concubine between courses.

Shango extended his hand and placed it on the young woman's arm. "I am Shango," he said.

While everyone in her group stopped what

they were doing, the young woman did not turn. She continued her conversation with a companion who had suddenly quit paying attention to her.

"I am Shango," the god repeated.

Without turning, the young woman reached for Shango's hand and removed it from her arm. "And I am in the middle of a conversation," she said, her back still to the God of Thunder.

Shango tried another tact. "My delicate flower," he said hoping his voice was no shaking. *What is happening to me*? he thought. He focused on the vision in front of him. "You are the loveliest creature I have ever seen. Your beauty exceeds that of any woman in the Kingdom of Abzu."

Again, without turning, she said, "And you need to try a compliment that I have not heard my entire life."

The roar came from deep within Shango, a primal protest of rage and indignation. "Do you know it is to whom you speak, girl?"

Silence fell on the banquet hall like a dropped hammer. No one moved – and if anyone breathed, it was very quietly. With a deliberation born of annoyance, the young woman turned – an agonizingly slow pivot of contempt.

"My Lord, first, in my culture, I am recognized as, and afforded every courtesy of, a woman. Secondly, but surely more important," here she made a mocking production of elaborate courtesy, "Everyone knows the great god Shango."

Shango beamed – momentarily.

"But, until this evening," she continued, "No one knew my Lord had manners worse than the man who slops the village pigs."

No one had ever dared speak with such insolence to Shango. He opened his mouth, a snarl poised on his lips. But the young woman spoke first.

"And I am not your delicate flower – or anyone else's. I am a huntress and a warrior in training. I can run, track, and handle weapons as well as a man – and better than most. If you want to gain my attention instead of my disdain, I suggest you work on a more creative approach."

One more time, Shango opened his mouth to speak.

He had no luck.

"Another thing," the woman said. "Take a bath. You smell worse than the dead animal that wore that hide before you did."

The young woman swept out of the room, three giggling maidens in her wake. No one laughed, but Shango heard a ripple of sniggers skitter through the crowd.

"Who the hell was that?" Shango said.

Even though he'd spoken to himself quietly, he heard a voice behind him.

"That, my Lord, is Nefertari – more properly, Princess Nefertari. She is the sister of King Gamba, younger by sixteen years. One day, she will be queen of Abzu."

**

Naomi had been Nefertari's lady-in-waiting

for years and she loved the Princess like a sister. Concern laced her voice.

"Are you all right, Your Grace? Your face is flushed, and you look like you have a fever?"

A voice behind them said, "She is fine, my dear."

Naomi turned to find Rehema, a woman who had known the Princess since birth. The older woman's eyes danced with mirth. "She is fine," she said again. "She just has *the fever*."

Naomi burst into tears. "Oh no, will she die?"

Rehema laughed. "Oh no, I think we can find a cure."

"What is it? Tell me. A root...a bush...the blood of a rhino? I will go kill one with my bare hands."

Rehema crossed the room to the Princess. "Your Grace, do you feel a little faint?"

"Yes."

"Are your cheeks burning?"

"Yes."

"Does it feel like your heart is going to pound out of your chest?"

"Yes."

Rehema lowered her voice a little.

"Do you ache between your legs?"

Nefertari shot to attention, her eyes wide. "How did you know that, Nurse? Tell me."

"As I said, Your Grace. You have the fever – the fever of love. You have met the man you will marry. Who is it?"

The Princess relaxed a little. "I have known I wanted him since the first time I saw him," she said. "I was a young girl when I saw him in battle. He was so handsome, so strong, so fearless."

Naomi began to laugh. "Aren't you the one who bragged how he would know who you were?" she asked.

"Yes," Nefertari said, "But I never thought he would ever speak to me."

Rehema patted her hand. "Who is this lucky man, my dear."

Nefertari stood and straightened her gown. "It is the God of Thunder. It is Shango."
**

"She is of age," Shango said. "I have inquired and discovered she underwent the ritual of fertility this time last year. She has not taken a husband because she claims there is no one to her liking."

Ogun sighed as he shook his head. "Just because she is of age does not mean she is old enough. The Elders on the High Council would not approve, not after the fiasco I endured."

"I said nothing about marriage," Shango said. "I just want that woman – I don't care how young she is." Then, he glared at his older brother. "Besides, why should you be allowed to wed a human and not me? I should have the right to marry any woman I want. I am Shango."

"That may work on the good citizens of Abzu, but not on me," Ogun said. "It will end badly. "And after my marriage, the High Council decreed we

21

could not marry humans. Let me tell you, it was very difficult not sharing the Great Secret."

Shango sneered and clenched his fist. "The members of the High Council can each put their shriveled lips on my muscular butt. Anyway – I need no one's permission."

"Have you forgotten about father?" Ogun asked. "He might want a say in the matter."

Shango shot Ogun a withering glance, then said, "I am a grown man. I do not need to ask our father to approve what I do."

Ogun tried hard to look displeased, but he started to chuckle. When he regained control, he put a heavy hand on his brother's shoulder. "Shango," he said, "You and I know we can do whatever we want while we are here – among these simpletons – but eventually, we will be recalled to our home. And we will be held accountable..."

Shango's disgust burned through the interruption. "*We* will be held accountable? You and I who are here in this mud pit, living in relative squalor while the lords of the High Council and our father, Emperor Anu, reside in luxury. They will do nothing to us as long as we bring in the gold they so desperately need."

Ogun could see the blood pulsing through the veins in Shango's neck. He knew better than to push the argument any further. He chose another tact.

"Shango, I do not think you can trust Nefertari. Humans are, by nature, very deceitful as my wife demonstrated."

Shango knew the truth – and he knew which of the couple had been deceitful – but now is not the time for that argument.

"If I decide to take the young girl, I will."

"She is of royal blood," Ogun said. "She is not one of the concubines you can ravish, then abandon. If you intend to have her, you will have to marry her. And here is the worst part."

"What is that?" Shango asked.

"You will have to ask her – and she will have to say yes of her own accord. This is nothing you can force simply because, as you love to say, you are Shango."

"Let's suppose that I did ask, and we did marry…"

Ogun interrupted, his face crisscrossed with mirth, "You ask, *then* she says yes, *then* you marry – assuming, of course, her brother, King Gamba approves."

Shango sneered. "That royal worm will do whatever I say. He may be ruthless, but he knows who has the real power."

Ogun shrugged and motioned for Shango to continue. "So," Shango said, "If I ask – and she says yes – and we marry – why do you think we might not be happy? That is, if I choose to be happy."

Ogun's laughter shook the room. "The woman cannot stand the sight of you," he said, tears cresting the corners of his eyes. "She thinks you are scum."

Shango waved his index finger in mock instruction. "You simply do not know the ways of women, dear brother."

Ogun was on his knees, laughing. "And…and… and she thinks you stink."

Shango flinched. He slowly raised his arm and sniffed.

"You know what?" he asked.

"What?" Ogun said now lying on his back trying to catch his breath.

"The woman is right." Shango stood from his throne. The room snapped to attention except for Ogun who was doubled over and cackling like a hyena. Shango swept his hand back and forth along a row of servants. "You, draw a bath – I want the water hot enough to remove my skin. You, bring three bags of the coarsest sand and three sponges. We will need to scrub. You, I want fragrant oils – but nothing that smells like a woman."

Ogun howled. "Or a dead animal!"

CHAPTER 3

Shango wasted little time. His pursuit began in earnest the next day.

"Deliver twelve dozen desert roses to the Princess immediately," he said.

"Yes, my Lord."

Before the servant turned to leave, Shango continued. "Not one of them will be withered or puny," he said. "They will be the finest anywhere. If even one is not perfect, I will hold you responsible. Is that clear?"

"At your command, my Lord," the servant said. "If there is so much as a small beetle on a single petal, I will end my own life."

Ogun rolled his eyes. "Brother Shango," he said. "Are you in that much need of relief? Look around. Over there (he gestured to the far wall) stand twenty of the most beautiful women in Azbu. They are the divine concubines – performing their religious service for one year. They have been trained by the most accomplished courtesans in the land. They will provide for your every need."

When Shango did not respond, Ogun continued. "We may not agree on everything, brother," he said, "But I know a particular area where we are of one mind – one thing we agree on."

Shango's nostrils flared in anticipatory anger. He hated when his brother claimed to *know* things. "What?" Shango asked.

"The women here," Ogun said. "Their love-making is spectacular. The act of coupling is invigorating – they are energetic. They want to please the Gods. And the moment of climax…"

He sighed and stared into space.

"In this case, you are correct, Brother Ogun. They are much more accomplished, interesting, and willing than the women of Nauru."

"You know, I hate the name of that place, brother," Ogun said, waving his hand in dismissal. "There, you are a soldier and I am a man of science. Here…" he paused reverently with his hand over his heart, "Here, we are gods."

Then, he cupped his crotch. "And stallions."

The brothers laughed.

"The blood of adventurers runs in our veins," Ogun said. "We have to have what we have to have."

Shango smirked at his brother. "You should know, Lord Ogun. You have sampled each one." Ogun's smile broke off when Shango said, "And most of them were not even yours. They were an offering to me. I should make you pay a fine."

Ogun frowned. "The women of Eleeka as – ah – lacking in certain ways," he said. "The female harvest here is much more bountiful. You should be honored to share with your older – and better looking – brother."

The brothers glared at each other – then, Shango chuckled. "You are so easily irritated, Ogun. Honestly, do you think I care? If you want one, take her with you when you return to Eleeka."

Ogun began perusing the women the way a cattle merchant assesses livestock. Then, Shango said, "Truly, I do not care, brother. Take them all."

Before Shango could change his mind, Ogun signaled several guards who herded the women out of a side door. "Thank you, brother," Ogun said. "I appreciate your generosity. How might I repay your great gift?"

Shango stared out at the sky. Without turning, almost as in a trace, he said, "Get Nefertari to fall in love with me."

CHAPTER 4

"Tell me a story, Grandfather." Omari's eyes gleamed with excitement. "I love your stories."

"Have you done your chores, Grandson," Dindaka asked.

"Yes, Grandfather."

"Including cleaning out the stables?"

The boy nodded vigorously. "Yes, Grandfather. You know, it is interesting."

"What is interesting."

"After a while, the smell of the manure is – well – it's almost pleasant."

The old man laughed softly. "Yes, child," he said even though he saw Omari's eyes narrow at the word *child*. "When you are older and travel to the distant lands, you will encounter that smell and it will remind you of home."

Neither spoke for a while, the old man in peaceful reminiscence, the youngster in mild bewilderment. Then...

"Grandfather...the story?"

Roused as if shaken from a nap, the old man began. "This is the Eleeka Legend," he said.

Face in hands, elbows on knees, Omari listened intently.

"The Eleekan people lived in peaceful seclusion in the Zambezi Valley for centuries. They had no contact with anyone else. They were simple folks who built their kraals along the banks of the great river and believed that their gods would supply all their needs.

"Their peace and solitude were shattered when they were told to leave their homes and move away from the river to avoid the flood that Ogun threatened to bring."

"Why would the God of War bring a flood, Grandfather?"

"It was about one of the third of the three great reasons – it was about a woman."

Omari nodded, trying to look wise. "Yes, women are the cause of much misery," he said.

"No, my grandson," Dindaka said. "They are the cause of much joy and the reason for much celebration. Men's lust for women – men's failure to understand women – that is what bring on so much unhappiness."

"What happened?"

Dindaka stared out of the door, his mind harkening to a time long ago. "It was many, many years before I was born," he said.

"Oooooooooh," Omari said. "I did not know anything happened that long ago. Was that before there was a sky?"

Dindaka looked quizzically at the lad, then realized he was being teased. He tousled the boy's hair and continued. "Ogun was married to the Ife, a beautiful and fiercely independent woman. She was from the Eleeka tribe though she had not lived among her people for many years. She had left to travel the world and to explore. While she was on her journey, she met Ogun and fell in love – at least she did. As you will learn when you grow older, some men – even gods – are incapable of fidelity."

Dindaka paused, anticipating interruption, but Omari was deeply attentive. The old man continued his story.

"They had great passion – and equally legendary fights. The War God was arrogant and thought himself above the constraints of marriage."

Omari sat up, eyes wide. "He took many women?" he asked.

"Crudely put," Dindaka said. "But woefully accurate. He was not a faithful husband. In addition to his dalliances, he was cruel and neglectful. His queen decided not to put up with him anymore."

"What happened? This is far more interesting than my school lessons," Omari said.

"No doubt," the old man said. "One day, Ogun returned to the mountain palace where they lived. He had been gone for three days in the company of five younger women. They were – ah – hunting."

Omari burst into laughter. "No, they were not, Grandfather. They were rutting like elephants in heat."

Now it was Dindaka's turn to laugh. "Do not let your mother hear you talking like that," he said.

"She will scrub your mouth the sand."

Omari, who had endured the punishment before – on several occasions – made a face.

Dindaka continued. "The Queen left a message for Ogun saying she was leaving him and taking refuge in Kush, the land of her birth. Kush was ruled by a goddess, Amma. She is the sister of Ogun and Shango – and she still rules Kush."

Omari nodded. "I remember that from my lessons."

"Good boy," Dindaka said. "To continue, Ife left a notice of divorce, a document stating that the marriage was at an end."

"Was Ogun sad and sorry for what he had done?"

The white head shook back and forth in denial. "Absolutely not. Ogun claimed he had the right to act as he pleased – he was, and is, after all, a god. He claimed the women were his rightful reward. He swore vengeance. 'In three days,' he said, 'I will destroy the great dam that hold back the waters of the Zambezi. I will bring a flood unlike any the world has ever seen. I will destroy your native land of Eleeka and every living being in it.'"

Omari scrunched his eyes. "Why would Ogun destroy his wife's country?" he asked. "Seems silly."

"It is an insane idea," Dindaka said, "While he had not been married to Ife but for a few years and though he had never bothered to visit the region of her birth, he knew she loved Eleeka have much. He had prohibited her from visiting – always came up with an excuse to keep her with him. But Ogun knew Ife's family still lived in Eleeka and he knew she loved them every much. She had grown up in that are – besides her parents and siblings, she knew almost everyone there. She was loved by the people and loved them in return. Ogun recognized that killing the people in Eleeka would wound his former wife."

"But the people and country of Eleeka are still there," Omari said.

"Yes," Dindaka said. "The day before the announced destruction of the dam, at Ife's urging, the goddess Amma, who had never liked Ogun – you know how brothers and sisters can fight – made a treaty with a powerful ally. They fought Ogun in a battle that raged for three days. Ife herself led a battalion of female warriors who distinguished themselves. The combined armies defeated Ogun and his forces. Alas, Ife was mortally wounded. Ogun rushed to her side, but she died before he made it."

Omari looked away and wiped the tears from his face, hoping his grandfather would not see.

"It is fine to weep, Omari," said the old man who knew and saw all things. "It is a tragic story of love and arrogance. So many people died because Ogun was not satisfied with the beautiful woman he had."

"What happened after she died, Grandfather?"

"Amma and her new strategic ally made Ogun sign a pact in which he swore on his life that he would do no harm to the people of Eleeka. It was a humiliating experience for the God of War to be bested by his wife, his sister, and her their supporter."

"Who was it that helped them, Grandfather?" Omari said. "Who helped to defeat the great God Ogun."

"That was the hardest thing for Ogun to tolerate," Dindaka said. "The person with whom Amma made the treaty was Ogun's own brother – the God of Thunder, Shango."

CHAPTER 5

From the family of Mensa, he'd been given the name Amani, which meant "trustworthy." When his father first looked on him, the smiling new parent said, "That is the face worthy of trust – he will be called Amani."

And he was – trustworthy. Far more responsible than his age, Amani grew. Though not as tall as some of the other soldiers, he was clever, strong, and exceptionally toned. His eyes were unusual. While almost all the men in Abzu had deep brown eyes, Mensa's were slate gray and could strike terror into the heart of even the most seasoned fighter.

Early in his teens he decided to shave his head – not something anyone else his age did but he felt it gave him a slight edge. A stray hair would never fall into his eye – staying clean was easier. Most important, in hand-to-hand combat, no enemy could gain an advantage by grabbing Mensa's hair.

He ran faster, jumped higher, fought longer, and worked harder than full-grown men. The youngest ever in his tribe to earn "warrior" status, he attracted attention from everyone.

The Mensa family was well respected; legend

said they descended from the original man, part of the Sand People. He'd heard the stories since boyhood: "Your father was a bodyguard – and your father's father before him." Such was his background, even if it was only partially true. While there were some, particularly among the very old, who knew the truth, no one wanted to risk death, so all Amani ever heard was, "Your father was a bodyguard…"

Amani did not remember is father very well. Jandal Mensa died – in battle (or so Amani was told) – long before the child reached the age of memory. But Amani had inherited his father's strength and the skill of all Mensa men.

The Mensa clan excelled in the ancient fighting arts. They were respected and beloved leaders. They were trained in land and sea fighting; they excelled on horseback; they were deadly stealth fighters and master tacticians. Legend said they received their power from the North Star. They took to the battlefield like children at play
**

One day, a stern-faced man interrupted Amani's meditation time.

"You are summoned," he said.

"Summoned where?" Amani asked.

"To the King's lodge."

"Summoned by whom?" Amani asked.

"Who else would summon you to the King's lodge, you idiot – the King – King Gamba."

When Amani entered the throne room, he

bowed low as he had been taught from an early age even though – as far as he knew – no one in his family had ever meet the King. "Your Highness," he said.

"Stand, son of Jandal, named Amani," King Gamba said. "I have a job for you."

Amani smiled. This, he liked. A royal assignment – to capture a lion, to battle an enemy, to scout for the warriors. "Anything, my King."

And that is how Amani of the House of Mensa came to guard the infant sister of the King.

"She will have her naming ceremony in two months," Gamba said. "From that moment until she is married, you will protect her with your life."

"I will guard her until I can guard no longer, my King," Amani said.

The young man knew all too well what he was saying. Should the Princess die while under this watch, he was obligated by honor to take his own life. When she died (even of natural causes) he would be buried in a smaller tomb next to hers, so he could protect her in the afterlife. Bodyguards could be spared by a royal decree, but such proclamations were rare – all monarchs wanted their entourage intact "on the other side of the river."

Amani Mensa endured rigorous training, more advanced than anything he'd ever previously endure. He bested men twice his age. He graduated at the top of his Academy class – just as had his father. Amani took the Oath of Allegiance at age twelve. His dedication ceremony took place two days before the Princess was named. At an elaborate service her brother's palace (followed by a week of feasting), the young girl was given the name "Nefertari" – "beautiful companion."

Every grandmother relayed the naming tradition.

"The Spirit of Death is always looking for new soldiers and handmaidens. But he can only take someone if he can call them by name. Babies and young children are weak. We must give them every chance, so we do not name a child until the fifth birthday, After that, their fate is in the hands of the gods."

Most young warriors would have been humiliated to be charged with watching *a girl*. Amani took to his new assignment with energy and enthusiasm. *If the King thinks enough of me to guard his sister,* he thought, *then I cannot do anything to betray that trust. I will shield her with my life.*

The Princess struggled to pronounce "Amani" – it came out "Nomnomi", but she had no problem with "Mensa." So, from about the second day of his assignment, the young warrior was known by everyone simply as "Mensa."

He spent every waking hour with the Princess, even standing in the same room when she bathed or changed clothes, albeit out of sight, standing quietly on the other side of a protective screen. Still, he was never more than three quick strides away from the young girl to whom he had pledged his loyalty and his life.

The relationship blossomed into a friendship, which had lasted for the last eleven years. He watched her with an affection born of purity of heart and a determination to service. His happiness was totally and exclusively determined by hers.

Mensa liked her within the first week. Nefertari was an intelligent and delightful child, full of life and energy. Though destined to become a great beauty, as a child she was cursed with a head full of uncontrollable hair. Her locks were so thick and curly that they defied combs and routinely escaped from any attempt at restraint. Most children would have developed a sensitivity, but Nefertari embraced her wild hair as part of her persona. Mensa enjoyed watching her play and dance; when she ran, her hair streamed behind her and she looked like a lion. When she sang, it sounded as if all of Nature had stopped to listen to her melodious voice.

By the time she was ten, Mensa was in love with the Princess. He would never act on his feelings – he would never tell anyone, though those closest to him could easily see how different he was, how Nefertari affected him. Mensa was a man of honor. He understood his responsibility – keep the Princess safe until the day of her wedding.

And beyond if she so requested.

Nefertari's parents had died shortly after her birth. Everyone told Nefertari that her father, King Akil, had died in hunting accident. Though she remembered her father a little, the memories faded with every day.

Mensa took every class with Nefertari, economics, battlefield tactics (even the women of Abzu knew how to fight), diplomacy, mathematics, and geography. In the stillness of the night, as Mensa half-slept just outside her door, he dreamed of ruling with Kingdom with Nefertari at his side – the adventures they would enjoy – the children they would bring into the world. But when the morning came, Mensa knew it had all been a foolish dream.

Nefertari told Mensa everything.

"I like a boy," she said one day. "He is the Prince of Jondu – his father is the King."

Shame crawled up Mensa's spine. He was not a prince; he was a lowly bodyguard. His thoughts of Nefertari were impossible, immature, and sometimes, impure. *She could never love me.* But, soon enough, Nefertari would say, "I have decided the Prince is a fool. He is not the one for me."

The news made Mensa's heart beat a little faster but not as rapidly as the day Nefertari announced, "I have decided I will never marry. I will become a warrior like the goddess Amma. I will lead my people into battle when necessary. In times of peace, I will be kind and generous. I may take a man when necessary (she always blushed when she said this, but Mensa pretended not to notice), but I will remain single my entire life. I do not need someone to look after me."

Mensa would not have been happier if someone had given him a herd of white elephants. Then, one day, one terrible day, Nefertari told him the second most awful thing he'd ever heard.

"Lord Shango has asked me to marry him."

Mensa felt woozy. For a moment, the world went out of focus. But he concentrated – he still had his duty. He could not allow any lapses. Then, Nefertari said the worst thing he'd ever heard.

"And I have decided to accept."

CHAPTER 6

Naomi's father, Xandia, served King Akil, the royal father to Gamba and Nefertari. Naomi's mother, Yanci, a woman of legendary beauty, was known as the greatest dancer in Abzu. When she was a younger woman, she performed at the wedding when Akil was married. According to legend, Yanci's dance was so elegant it caused grown men to weep and so erotic that the newly-wedded Queen pulled the King to the wedding chamber within three minutes of its conclusion. Their passion echoed throughout the palace. When they returned to the ongoing feast two hours later, they were applauded.

So grateful was Akil, he engaged Yanci to dance regularly to inspire his wife, that he gave Xandia and Yanci a home of their own – one next to the royal residence. The mansion came with a host of servants who provided everything for the couple who quickly became the King's favorites.

Little Naomi routinely played in the royal garden, a delightful place that housed all manner of exotic plants and animals. One of the featured attractions were the Butterflies of Barza – giant beasts whose wingspan exceeded four feet. Though delicate in appearance, the flying insects had been trained to ferry small children on their backs. When they were not soaring around the garden, they would stand patiently and await passengers. Both Naomi and her little sister, Eja, loved to "ride the flies."

Naomi has received careful instruction. She knew how to handle the giant creatures, how to make them follow her every instruction. She knew their abilities and their limitations. She also knew to avoid the Stingers. Tall, green, and serene-looking, the Stingers were massive, eight-foot plants featuring brightly colored pods atop their stalks. The vivid colors attracted mosquitoes, flies, beetles, and other critters that might harm either human beings or the beautiful plants in the garden. When an unsuspecting wasp lit on the exotic pod, it opened, exposing sharp, needle-like prongs. The movement was as quick as a cat and as lethal as a cobra.

The garden was vermin-free.

One day, Naomi and Eja went to the garden. Naomi was tired – too tired to keep up with her energetic baby sister. Naomi decided to lie down next to the coy pond and rest.

"Do not ride until I awaken," she said.

"Yes, sister," Eja said. But when one of the giant butterflies touched down right next to her, she could not resist. She mounted and took flight.

The butterfly, by instinct, knew better than

to fly close to the Stingers, but it was also trained to follow the instructions of whomever was on its back. Eja whooped and hollered and shrieked in delight as she put the butterfly through a series of loops, rolls, and dives. Not paying attention, she pulled out of a maneuver and steered directly into the Stingers.

Naomi awoke to Eja's shrieks for help. By the time the guards hacked the child out of the tangle of attacking plants, Eja has suffocated. Xandia and Yanci never recovered. After the accident, they remained inside their home where the King saw to their every need. Yanci never danced again – both she and her husband died of broken hearts within two years of the tragedy. Since neither of the bereaved parents could care for Naomi, Akil and his bride took her under their protection.

Naomi was assigned as a companion for the young princess, who had yet to undergo her naming ceremony. Thus, Naomi and Nefertari became fast friends and lifelong companions.

Three years older than Nefertari, Naomi was immediately attracted to Mensa, the handsome, young body guard assigned to the Princess. Naomi adored him, dreaming about him constantly and pining for his attention. But Mensa only had eyes for Nefertari.

CHAPTER 7

Even the most dedicated guards took time off – it was required. Gamba understood how difficult it was to stay alert all the time – he was a brilliant soldier and warrior in his own right. All the guards had mandatory days of rest. Mensa always balked when his "down time" came, but the Captain of the Guard was adamant.

"You will take your time, Mensa."

"No one can guard the Princess as I can, sir."

The Captain was amused. *Poor boy has no idea everyone knows he is in love with the Princess.* But since he knew Mensa was a man of honor who would never sully his name or Nefertari's reputation, he said, "While that may be true, the regulations are clear. I have learned you skipped your last two periods of rest. You will not ignore this one."

Mensa hung his head. "I was only trying to do my duty."

In a rare lapse of his stern façade, the Captain placed a hand on Mensa's shoulder. "I understand, Mensa. You honor your family's legacy. You are the best soldier and fighter I have. But how would you feel if something happened to the Princess because you were a quarter of a heartbeat slow – what if you were wearier than you knew. Surely you understand that the clumsiest fox can occasionally sneak past a drowsy farmer."

Mensa bit his lip. "I have never considered that before, sir. From now on, I will be diligent in taking my time for renewal – I will consider it part of my training."

One evening, when he was away from the Princess, Mensa fell asleep at the edge of the valley. He'd trained all day in the heat, pushing himself, seeing how far he could run without stopping, how long he could fight through the desert heat without water. When he lay down for a rest, the Goddess of the Night dropped an entire bag of dream dust on him.

The vision came suddenly and would not depart. Snakes of all kinds slid and slithered throughout his subconscious. He wrestled with constrictors and dodged vipers. Whenever he would defeat one serpent, three more would take its place. Soon, he could not move without stepping on one. They were striking and grasping his limbs, pinning him down; he heard his ancestors making a deal for his life, offering his soul so he might live.

He awoke with a sweaty start. He reached for his flagon of water, drained it, and began to run. He covered the five miles to his grandmother's hut in record time. Efia was pleased to see her beloved grandson and covered his head with kisses even as she fussed at how thin he had become.

The tantalizing odors of roast lamb and baking bread filled the hut. Mensa realized he was famished, and he ate until he was more than stuffed. The discomfort of his full belly was offset by the joy he had at seeing his grandmother.

"It has been too long, my son," Efia said.

"Yes grandmother, I am sorry. But ..."

Efia held up a hand. "There is no need to explain," she said. "Your father was an elite guard and his father before him. I know the life. You are doing your duty." The lie , told so long and so regularly, came to the old woman with such ease, Mensa never thought to question it.

Mensa nodded and stared into the fire.

"What is troubling you, my son?"

Mensa continued gazing at the embers. Finally, he turned to see his grandmother's sad eyes. They had carried the weight of pain and anguish as long as Mensa could remember. Even when she laughed, her eyes looked ready to weep.

"I had a dream, Grandmother," he said. "It upset me very much."

"There is no reason for you to be burdened, child," she said. "Tell me the dream."

He told her. When he was finished, she was quiet for a very long time. He knew better than to break the silence.

Finally, she spoke. "My son," she said, "You did not have a dream; you had a vision. It is time for you to know the truth."

CHAPTER 8

Mensa felt like his head was going to explode.

"What do you mean we were the royal family?"

Efia looked into his eyes – a deep, penetrating gaze. Mensa felt her eyes burning into his core. "You can never speak of this, my son," she said. "There is a Royal Censure."

"A what?"

"It is a decree from the King. Though there are not many left who know, anyone who speaks of this will be instantly put to death. No trial. No witnesses. Just immediate execution."

"This comes from Gamba?" Mensa asked. "That does not seem possible. He is a good and fair king – a man of honor and…"

Efia's harsh laughter stopped the young soldier mid-sentence. "Gamba, the good? Gamba, the fair? You might as well call him Gamba, the flying monkey," Efia said. "He is a snake, a dangerous asp, venomous and cunning. And he is a coward. He will always choose to attack from the rear, to bite you in the heel. Facing someone man-to-man is not anything that ever crosses his weasel's mind. He and his kin are the snakes of your vision."

"But he is Nefertari's brother," Mensa said, his voice rising in protest. "And she is..."

Again, the shrill cackle. "I know, I know. She is good and kind and lovely and smells like honeysuckle. Boy, she could have five heads and spit manure and you would never say an unkind word about the woman you love."

Mensa lowered his head but did not speak.

Efia could see the confusion in Mensa's eyes. "What is troubling you, my son?" she asked.

"You know?"

"Everyone knows," Efia said. "You have been moony-eyed over that girl since the first day you saw her."

The young man stood in irritation, "Grandmother, I would never..."

Her stern eyes cut him off and drove him back onto the cushion. "I am sorry, Grandmother," he said. "I should never raise my voice to you."

"You are forgiven, my son," she said. "I did not say you had done anything wrong, but I have known – we have all known since you were a boy – that you love the Princess."

Mensa hung his head. "Yes, I have loved her for as long as I can remember."

He was going to raise another fierce protest of his innocence, but he knew the old woman understood. It was time for him to be quiet and to listen.

Efia stared at the fire for a while. "You do not know what to do and you need guidance, correct?"

"Yes."

"Who is the wisest man in the Kingdom?"

"Dindaka. He is the wisest man in the world."

Efia laughed. "And he is vain enough to love it when people call him that. He is certainly among the wisest, I will grant him that. His very name means 'Sea of Knowledge,' as you know. But there are other wise ones."

"Who?"

"Dindaka comes from the clan of the Magi, ancient philosophers and astrologers. They read the secrets that are written in the stars – they understand the secret language of the night skies. Every member of that clan is brilliant and learned. They have been so since the first god made the first man."

Mensa bit his lip. "Grandmother, if there is a royal ban, why would Dindaka tell me anything?"

Efia reached out her hand. "Dindaka has taken the oath of Mangus, the first Magi. Dindaka is sworn always to tell the truth. It is an oath of honor and an oath of blood. Whether he likes it or not, whether it is best for him personally or not, Dindaka will always – always – tell the truth. And whenever you are ready, Dindaka will tell you the rest of the story."

CHAPTER 9

"He sends flowers and gifts every day, Nurse."

The Princess put her nose close to the dazzling array of orchids and drew in a deep breath. "Yesterday he sent these." She touched a stunning strand of pearls around her neck. "All those years ago, I never thought he would know who I am."

Rehema's hand rested lightly on Nefertari's arm. "What is it you want to do, child?"

"I want to be his wife."

The old woman exhaled slowly. "You know it is forbidden. He is a god. You are human."

"Yes. What should I do – what can I do?"

Rehema stood as she patted the arm of the girl she loved like her own daughter. "I do not know, my dear. But if you follow you heart, I know this will all work out."

**

The wedding announcement met with mixed reactions. Nefertari had accepted and then informed her brother the King. Gamba could not have been any more stunned if someone had hit him with a chariot axle.

"Are you sure?" he said. "There are countless

warriors and lords who would do anything to marry you."

"I am sure, my brother," she said. "I have loved Shango for a long time." Seeing the dark cloud pass across Gamba's face, she said, "I have never acted on my feelings, brother. That is not my way. I would never do anything to bring shame on our family."

Gamba nodded but his raised eyebrow indicated skepticism.

Nefertari was adamant. "I will be a maiden on my wedding night, O King. Of that I promise you."

The King relaxed. "My primary concern is for you, my beloved sister."

Your primary concern is for your precious reputation, dear brother, she thought. Still, she smiled. "I think we will be very happy."

"I hope so, sister. I most certainly hope so."

But in his mind, the King fretted about the consequences of a royal union with one of the gods.

The Elders responded in mixed fashion. Uduru, her face pale and sweaty, shrieked her disapproval. "We will pay dearly for this blasphemy."

Runako of the Hill People gave a long speech. He finished by saying, "Marrying a God will bring tragedy to our lives. We have obeyed the divine laws for many harvests; now we break them. We all know what happens when we break the rules; the Universe begins to spin out of balance. It did once before and almost resulted in the destruction of Eleeka."

Dindaka approached the situation with his

characteristic calm. "Brothers and sisters, we cannot foretell the future. Just because no one has ever married a god for a long time does not mean this wedding will bring destruction. We live in a new day – a new era – a time when the gods and the people have more interaction. In my boyhood, we stared at the gods from a distance, never daring to speak or to gesture. Just last month, every person here reveled at a party at Shango's home. Was it blasphemy to drink his wine? If so, Runako, you committed multiple infractions. By my count, you, your wife, and your sons polished off an entire cask by yourselves. I saw no outrage that evening. Shango is our protector. This marriage guarantees he will be concerned with our wellbeing. Let this play out – I believe in my heart that everything will be fine."

Without ever raising his voice, Dindaka calmed the storm and restored order.

**

On the other side of the Great Mountains, Ogun was not pleased. He hurled a vase across his throne room. The pottery disintegrated just behind General Tyreek's head.

"That fool brother of mine will undermine our power," he said. No one moved to oppose him. The members of the court knew better than to challenge Ogun's rage. Those who had tried in the past were never seen again. "We have tried to marry humans before – it was a disaster."

Against his better judgment, General Tyreek

decided to speak. He wanted to calm Ogun before things got out of hand. "Perhaps, my Lord, things will work out better for him than they did…"

The General did not finish the sentence. He could not – Ogun held him two cubits[3] off the ground by the throat. About the time Tyreek began to turn blue, Ogun released him.

"Do you still think the marriage is a good idea, General?"

"No, my Lord," Tyreek said as he rasped for air. "It is a terrible idea."

"Precisely," Ogun said. "No human can ever again get so close to the Great Secret. If they discover we are not divine, we will lose our power."

Tyreek's bloodlines stretched deep into Eleekan history. No one could remember a time when anyone other than a member of his family headed the national army. He was an ungainly man – looking several inches too tall for his frame as if he'd been hung from a tree limb as a youngster. His torso was oddly elongated, and his wrists stretched to his knees. Though he continually carried himself with a military bearing, his bizarre anatomy and splotchy beard gave him a slightly unkempt look. The hair on his chin looked like a thick bush that had been attacked by beetles – lush in places, almost non-existent in others. The hair on his head suffered from the same affliction. Strangely dull, reddish-tinted brown eyes completed his unusual appearance.

Still, those who underestimated his brilliant mind did so at their own peril. It had taken a while for the General to gain Ogun's trust, but the bond between the two men was now unbreakable. Tyreek was devoted – and Ogun trusted him completely.

Tyreek continued to swipe shards from his tunic as he choked. "What would you have me do, my Lord?" he asked. "I could send a cohort of my men to disrupt the wedding. They could go disguised as guests, then cause a commotion – start a fight or something – right in the middle of the service. If necessary, if I may be so bold, should you order it, perhaps the young princess could have... um ... an accident – perhaps a fatal one – as a result. We would, of course, eliminate the men chosen for the assignment. No one will ever know they came from your kingdom.

Ogun stroked his chin. "Your idea has merit, General," he said. "But I fear my brother might recognize our unique fighting skills, those things that take over by instinct. Were he to determine our responsibility, nothing would stop him from seeking to destroy us. No, we will wait. This has been a long time coming. Ever since my brother teamed with my scheming ex-wife to stymie my plans, I have intended to punish him. Now, he presents me with the perfect opportunity. I will attend the wedding and play the happy brother. My joy will lull him into a false sense of security. When he least expects it, we will strike, and I will have my vengeance."

CHAPTER 10

On the day of the wedding, dignitaries arrived from all over the world. The kings and queens of Timbuktu and Benin. The queen of Kush send her profound regrets with a personal message.

> *Dearest Brother, while I would love to celebrate your wedding with you, I fear my presence would upset our sibling, Ogun. I do not wish for him to make a scene. He still holds great resentment over the issue with Yanci and the Eleekan people. Know that I rejoice in your happiness and will hold good thoughts for you and your bride. By reputation, she is a ravishing beauty. As your older sister, I admonish you to show her great affection and respect – certainly more than our brother did for his earthly bride. This can be the start of something wonderful for you – or something tragic for the world we rule. Make wise choices. Love, Amma*

The note came in a box from which glimmered a stunning gold and emerald necklace. Other nations sent high-ranking officials. Everyone brought extravagant gifts.

Pyramids of ivory, exotic spices, gold, iron, copper, ebony, and cotton threatened to take over the palace even as more and more tribute came through the palace doors. The representative from Punt brought four black leopards, each wearing a diamond-studded collar. Every nation tried to out-do the next.

Still, there was an undercurrent of dis-ease in the crowd. No one knew exactly what it meant for a human woman to marry a god. The union would make Nefertari a human goddess – the first in a long time. Her power would exceed that of any other earthly monarch.

War was a real possibility. Whispers ran through the crowd. They took different forms, but all carried basically the same frightened (and fright-ening) concern. "When will Ogun attack?"

The morning of the ceremony Shango sent gifts to Nefertari's brother – robes, jewelry, luxuri-ous rugs and tapestries, and a truck of silver. (Gold was prohibited in any trade or as a gift. It was the sacred offering to the gods – only gods could wear it. Amma's gift to Nefertari symbolized acceptance of the human woman into the divine atmosphere.)

Eight of Shango's personal bodyguards (en-gaged more for show that for protection – the God of Thunder was very capable of defending himself) marched to King Gamba's palace to escort the Prin-cess to the wedding. As Nefertari walked out, two of the guards poured a libation of the finest wine onto the ground.

"May this offering serve as a blessing to you and your union for the rest of time!"

They repeated the process at intervals along the route. While the ritual grew a little tedious to the young woman who was eager to be about the business of getting married, she appreciated the gesture and reminded herself to find a special way (she had been receiving instruction from Rehema on the ways of pleasuring men) to thank her husband.

Ogun entered with a retinue of guards and "guests." "I have never seen so many beautiful women," one of the attendees said. He received a whispered response, "I think that is what Lord Ogun's bed chamber looks like every night of the week."

Ogun wore a long robe of brocaded silk. Gold leaf shimmered from every border of the garment to remind anyone who might forget about his divine nature. His massive, oiled shoulders gleamed in the sunlight. He looked like the sun itself.

Men, even proficient and fearless warriors, scurried out of Ogun's path lest they incur his wrath. Scores of unattached women lingered as long as they dared, hoping to catch the god's eye and to be invited to join his entourage. A night with Ogun offered a tantalizing double edge – a woman's reputation could be forever ruined – or she could find herself promoted to Chief Consort and live the rest of her life in luxury. It was a chance many women were inclined to take – much to Ogun's lust-ful delight.

By the time Nefertari reached Shango's, the party was in full swing. Smiling Fula women balanced calabashes on their heads as they swayed to rhythmic music. Muscular percussionists thumped out an intoxicating pattern on their drums. The crowd, already well lubricated from Shango's wine casks, whirled and swirled in every direction. But every thump stopped, every instrument fell quiet, and every dancer froze when the herald announced, "Lords, ladies, and assembled guests, her Royal Highness, Princess Nefertari."

The wedding was the thing of legends. Resplendent in a high-necked, white gown, the Princess walked into the hall, a thirty-cubit[4] train trailing her like a silken river. Her hair was swept up in a high bouffant. A crown of silver and diamonds caressed her forehead. Green eyelid paint set her eyes ablaze against her caramel skin and accented her emerald eyes; the tint on her full lips matched the ornamentation of her eyes.

Shango's bare, oiled dark chest tapered into a full skirt of crimson silk. Leather straps studded with gold (only gods were allowed or own or wear the sacred element) crisscrossed his muscular torso and held his razor-sharp battle ax against his back. No mere mortal could lift the weapon, but Shango carried it as if it were a small, weightless child.

After the procession music echoed away,

Nefertari's only living relative, King Gamba, gave a short speech and surrendered control and protection of the Princess to the "care and benevolence" of Shango.

When Shango lifted Nefertari's veil, she gasped – she was always awestruck by the god's masculine beauty. Taller than anyone she had ever imagined his jet-black hair fell in dreadlocks to his massive shoulders. Most men would wish for their legs to be a large and precisely-defined as Shango's arms. His thigh, which stuck out through a slit in his wedding garment, approximated the trunk of a Baobab tree. His almond colored eyes reflected the candlelight in a way Nefertari found intoxicating. Though she was still a maiden and had never known a man, she felt desire pulsing through her.

The priest droned through the ceremony. When he finally pronounced "man and wife," the party erupted, resuming where it had been suspended. Even though the bride and groom left after the first few toasts, the celebration continued without them for three full days.

**

"I want to show you something," Shango said.

"I have been told what to expect, my Lord – you do not need to give me any previews," Nefertari said. When Shango looked at her quizzically, Nefertari giggled. "I may be a virgin, my Lord, but I am not a prude."

Shango's booming laugh echoed off the outside walls of the palace. "Very good, wife," he said.

"Very good. But that comes later. Now, I want you to see something no human has ever seen before."

He guided her around the corner. His silver dragon rested on the portico.

Nefertari stopped in her tracks. "I have seen this before," she said. "But never this close. Is it safe for me to approach?"

Shango put a reassuring hand on her shoulder. "As long as you are with me, you are safe," he said.

Despite Nefertari's halting steps, Shango led her into the beast's belly.

This is a very strange animal, Nefertari thought. *It is unlike anything I have ever seen. The skin shines in the sun like a sword and the insides are hollow.*

As the dragon lifted into the sky, Nefertari marveled at the bright lights and symbols that flashed inside the creature. Though she had heard tales of dragons and seen the ones that belonged both to Shango and Ogun, she had never been this close – much less "swallowed." A portal opened in the monster's side. Nefertari moved hesitantly closer to it and peered out. She gasped as she realized how high from the ground they were – higher – much higher than the treetops – and moving faster than a cheetah.

The savannah stretched out below them. She saw all manner of beasts – she recognized them all – but they were small as if in miniature. She saw Kampala – the legendary rogue elephant – one spotted about once a year when it rampaged through a hapless village. It looked less imposing than a house cat.

Nefertari let out a shriek of delight. Shango's only response was to move his hands over some of the lights. The dragon's speed doubled.

Nefertari looked deeply into her new husband's eyes. "Shango," she said. "You are, indeed, a god."

**

Mensa slid away so quietly that it took Nefertari several minutes to recognize she was – for the first time in her life – in a room alone with another person. Shango stood by the window, the moon spotlighting his nakedness. His muscles rippled even when he was motionless. When he turned to her, Nefertari gasped a little.

"Are you displeased, my love?" he asked.

"N-n-no, my Lord," she said. "I have just…"

"You have never been with a man before," he said. "I understand. That probably means you have never seen a man naked."

Nefertari hung her head a little. "No, my Lord."

"But you have been instructed?"

"Yes, my Lord."

Shango came closer and put his hand on Nefertari's shoulder. Very slowly, very softly, he guided the strap of her gown off her left shoulder – then the other – until the silk fell from her body and she stood before him nude.

"I want you to do something for me," he said.

"I know my place, my Lord. I am to please

you. What would you have me do?"

She reached from him. She started to kneel, as Rehema had suggested but Shango put his hands under her arms and lifted her.

"Actually, I want two things," he said.

"Yes, my Lord."

"The first is to forget everything anyone told you, taught you, or suggested to you. We are husband and wife. Together, we will explore and learn. You know my past – you know I have been with many concubines, but those situations were for sport – for relaxation – for clearing my mind. I have never been with anyone for love – and I do love you."

It was the first time Shango had ever said that phrase. Nefertari's heart pounded in her chest and she broke into a broad smile. Shango continued.

"We will learn how to please one another – equally. Your joy will be mine and mine will be yours. Does that sound good?"

"Yes, my Lord," she said. "And what is the other, my Lord?"

Shango smiled in the moonlight. His teeth gleamed and his eyes danced. "The second, wife, is that you quit calling me 'My Lord.' In public, where there is protocol and stuffiness, we will observe the traditions of your people. In here – any time we are alone – I only want to be one thing."

"What is that, my Lord?"

Shango laughed, full and deep. "I think you are mocking me," he said.

"A little, my Lord," she said. "Seriously, what would you have me call you?"

"I am your husband. I want to be the love of your life. Find someone to call me – but not my Lord."

"I will call you 'husband.'"

"The most wonderful word I have ever heard," he said.

He took Nefertari in his arms and kissed her softly. He had to lift her a little as he was a full two cubits[5] taller, but the kiss remained tender and gentle until Nefertari opened her mouth to him. Then they kissed with great passion.

Nefertari gasped and wrapped her legs around Shango's waist. He laid her gently on the bed and positioned himself. As he entered her, she cried out.

"Are you in pain, my love," he asked stopping and pushing away.

She reached for him and pulled him closer. "It is joy, husband – it is joy."

CHAPTER 11

One year after the wedding...

What began with such promise quickly developed issues – one specific issue. A young woman in the prime of her life, Nefertari wanted a child – she wanted many children. Despite coupling with her husband in exquisite passion several times a day, her monthly curse appeared with frightening regularity.

"Why are you so quiet this morning, wife?" Shango asked. "Did I not please you last evening?"

"You always please me, my lord husband," she said. "You have the reputation for ferocity. No one would ever suspect how tender you are in the marriage bed."

Shango put a finger to his lips and made a great show of looking around the room. He even peered under the dining table as if suspicious someone was hiding there.

"Do not speak so loudly, my beloved," he said as he chuckled. "You will ruin my image."

Nefertari smiled wanly.

"Still," Shango said. "You have not told me what is wrong."

"You know, husband," she said with a sigh. "I

am still not with child. I must be doing something wrong."

Shango shook his vigorously. "Not at all, my flower. You are enthusiastic – and becoming quite skilled. You now make love like a highly-trained concubine."

He dodged the coconut aimed at his head. "It was meant as a compliment," he said.

"You need to work on your flattery," she said. Her voice was flat, but her eyes danced with delight at their teasing. She grew serious. "But I am worried. I want a baby."

"You know it cannot happen," he said. "The gods cannot have children with humans. I have been told it is not possible."

"We were *forbidden* to marry," she said. "That did not stop us."

Shango fell into a deep silence. Nefertari knew her husband. He was preparing to reveal more about his background – something he did in little dribbles of information from time to time. She waited patiently. He would speak when he was ready.

She did not realize the things he would eventually tell her would shatter everything she knew ... or thought she knew.

CHAPTER 12

A time long, long before...

"The operation is very impressive, Dr. Bondu."

Emperor Anu, father of Ogun and Shango, towered above the diminutive scientist. While Bondu was the intellectual superior of every person in the Empire of Nauru, the mere mention of Anu's name struck fear into the heart of anyone who heard it. The Emperor's reputation as a fearless warrior and heartless ruler was well-earned. Though he was a visionary leader, he possessed a vicious streak that put everyone on edge in his presence.

"Thank you, my Liege," Bondu said. "From this moment on, every birth in the Empire will be at your direction. We have captured all the genetic material in the Empire and sterilized every physically mature citizen. When a male child comes of age, and we will know as we monitor each adolescent citizen for nocturnal emissions, we will bring him in, siphon off his seed, operate and render him perpetually infertile."

Anu rubbed his groin subconsciously. "You are not making eunuchs of my citizens, are you?"

"They will still function as always, my Lord. They will just – I believe the crass expression is – shoot blanks. They will be incapable of impregnating a woman."

"And what of the women?"

The Emperor continued to gaze at the gleaming lab. It was equipped with every conceivable piece of scientific equipment – the most sophisticated bio-genetic facility in the Universe.

"After the onset of her flow, every maiden is required to present herself to the lab. We also monitor every family's refuse. We know when women are in their cycle."

The Emperor shuddered. He'd seen more blood than any other warrior on the planet. He was fearless on the battlefield. But the thought of a woman's "time" still made him squeamish.

"Go on."

"We harvest every egg we can find, then tie the tubes of fertility."

"Why not take out the ovaries?"

"Young women need to hormones, my Lord, you know – ah – to – ah – develop."

"Ah, yes. We want shapely, well-built women in the realm. Good thinking."

Cretan, Bondu thought, just before he remembered...

...the backhanded blow caught the scientist just under his right jawbone and sent him sprawling. His head slammed into the far wall. Stars erupted in front of his eyes. It took a full minute for him to re-

67

orient.

"Do not forget, Bondu," the Emperor said, "that even though you are far smarter, I am far stronger. And, I can read your very thoughts."

I never...

"I know, my dear doctor. You never should have invented the Mind Sweeper. But I thank you. Though it only functions in close proximity, I am the only individual in the known universe who has one. It makes me unbeatable both on the field of combat and in the arena of political intrigue. As long as I know what others are thinking, no one can defeat me – no one can plot against me."

"A thousand pardons, my Lord. Sometimes, I do not control myself very well."

Anu extended a hand and picked Bondu up from the floor.

"You are forgiven. Just be prudent – and remember your place."

"Yes, Lord."

"Turning back to the subject at hand – how do we determine pregnancies and how do we regulate population growth? We must be careful as the atmosphere grows continually thinner. The precious gold we breathe becomes increasingly rare. No one realized our atmosphere was finite."

"Yes, sire," Bondu said. "That is why we continue sending out exploration parties. They find other planets and search for gold."

Anu interrupted. "Are you making progress on the atomizer?"

"It is finished, sire," Bondu said. "When the shipments of gold arrive from our colonies, we will load it in my device – it is mammoth, and I am quite proud of it. Would you care for a tour some day?"

I would rather have all my teeth extracted than listen to this egghead drone on and on about his inventive genius, the Emperor thought. But he said, "Perhaps, doctor, if I can ever find time away from the affairs of the Empire."

"Certainly, my Liege," the scientist said. "Suffice it to say, it works wonderfully. As I said, we load the gold, it goes through a process of de-molecularization, which renders it into a fine mist. We introduce it into our atmosphere with great precision, being careful not to disturb the elemental balance of the air we breathe. Gradually, we will restore the original ratios and our planet's future will be safe. If..." He paused.

"If, what?"

"If the exploration parties continue to send gold in sufficient quantities."

Anu mused quietly, chewing the inside of his mouth. "Yes," he said. "My sons are in charge of the most promising site – they will not fail us."

"No, my Lord. I am sure they will not." Bondu waited for the Emperor to reply. When he did not, the scientist continued with the original conversation. "To date, we have been very successful, but keeping pace with the population is difficult. Every year, your High Council sets the population number. It is, as you know, based on an algorithm I designed that accounts for the age of our citizens and projected death rate. We have factors for accidental death, accidents with our expeditionary forces, and … ah … executions. We are replacing at a 58% rate. For every 100 citizen who die, we produce only 58, thus reducing strain on our planet's resources."

"We can change that replacement number at any time?"

"Yes, my Lord. And, as you know, birthers – the woman who carry the fetuses – are very carefully selected for their sturdiness. A special Task Force of the High Council hand picks parents based on genetic factors. We are, in truth, growing a race of super beings."

The Emperor narrowed his eyes. "I can read your thoughts, Bondu, but your massive brain is racing so fast, I cannot keep up. What else do you want to tell me."

The scientist lowered his head. He was always reluctant to give his master anything approaching bad news. "I fear, my Lord, that as the generations progress, as women become more and more aware of their complete inability to conceive, their natural desire for coupling will diminish and eventually disappear."

"You are saying the female members of our race will not longer want to have sex?" Bondu cringed in expectation of an explosion. Instead, the Emperor smiled.

"That is fine," Anu said. "Most of our woman are, at best, unenthusiastic. We will take our pleasure with the females we import from our excursions."

"I am relieved you are not disappointed, my Lord."

"Why would I be upset, Bondu. It is not like you have rendered me impotent. I will always have a readily available supply of women for my needs."

Bondu was quiet for a while, staring at his lab – the lab of his dreams. He knew better than to think – anything – but he had questions. He always had questions about this work.

Finally – "My Lord?"

"Yes."

"What if someone conceives?"

"According to you, it is not possible."

Bondu nodded. "In theory, that is true, my Lord. But there are always variables in science. Perhaps something will happen and one of our Nauruians will be with child."

A strange smile creased the Emperor's face – a crooked smile – a wicked ... no ... evil smile.

"If that happens, Bondu, it is a crime against the State," he said. "Everyone involved will be put to death. Everyone including the incompetent scientists who allowed it to happen."
**

Shango did not tell Nefertari any of this. If she knew, she would also know the Deep Secret.

CHAPTER 13

The servant fell to his knees, forehead to the ground.

"Speak," Shango said

"Your Lordship, the Princess is unwell."

Shango was out of bed and sprinting for the bath before the servant could finished the explanation. Nefertari was on the floor, wrapped like a serpent around a copper basin.

"My love! Are you ill?"

Nefertari retched into the basin, but when she lifted her head, though pale, she was smiling.

"No, my husband," she said. "I am not ill."

"But you are vomiting and weak. Was it something you ate? I will have the cook punished."

"No, husband. It was not anything I ate."

"You have been bitten by a scorpion? Stung by a wasp?"

"I have been speared by my husband?"

Shango stood erect. "I did not spear you, my love. I would never raise my hand against you – I would never attack you with a weapon."

Nefertari smiled – she looked a little grim, but she did her best. "No, husband. You lanced me with your manhood – a most regular and pleasant experience. Apparently, you were a little more effective on one occasion."

"You mean I gave you more pleasure? Tell me what I did, and I will do it again."

Now, Nefertari laughed. "You may be a god, but you are a silly, silly man. Every time with you is heavenly, husband. But apparently, on one of our encounters within the past few months, you accomplished more than making me scream in delight."

Shango stared at her like a baboon looking in a mirror.

"I do not understand."

"Silly man," she said. "Silly Shango. Husband, love of my life – I am pregnant. We are going to have a baby!"
**

Shango called for his dragon, mounted, and took to the sky. Within minutes, he landed at Command Headquarters. General Takai leapt to his feet and bowed his head.

"My Lord, why are you here? I would have come immediately if you had summoned."

"Where is Mensa – he is not on guard."

"Training, my Lord, in the River Valley. Mandatory for all soldiers. We must maintain readiness in case of an attack."

"Give me his exact coordinates."

After several minutes of frantic communication, Takai handed Shango a slip of papyrus. "He is here, my Lord."

Shango turned and headed for the door. He stopped and spoke over his shoulder. "General, arrange for someone else as my wife's full-time bodyguard."

"My Lord?

"Before the sun sets, Mensa will die."

**

The dragon landed with fire and noise. The craft could have settled silently; it had full stealth capacity, but Shango knew how the roar and flames intimidated the locals. The Captain of the Guard approached, quaking.

"My Lord Shango," he said bowing low.

"Where is Mensa?"

"I shall summon him, my Lord."

Shango's backhand lifted the Captain off ground and sent him sprawling. "If I wanted you to send for him, I would have commanded it. Where is he?"

Five minutes later, Shango strode over the crest of a low hill. Mensa was supervising weapons training. When he saw Shango, he rushed over and bowed.

"My Lord," he said. "Is the enemy attacking?"

"No."

"Why are you here?"

Shango drew himself to his full height and reached back for his axe. Drawing the menacing weapon from its harness, he said, "You know full well why I am here, you traitorous scum."

Mensa flinched at the insult. "My Lord, you

have no more loyal servant. I have served you as I serve your wife…"

Shango roared at the mention of Nefertari. "You mean as you serviced my wife. You have slept with my woman and fertilized her with your inferior seed. Now, you will die."

Mensa did not flinch this time. He stood his ground and looked Shango in the eye. "No, my Lord. I did not – I would never betray you or defile Nefertari in that manner. Whoever told you that is a liar and I will deal with him."

"You will deal with me," Shango said assuming a fighting stance. "And it will be the last time you ever deal with anyone."

Shango lunged, swinging his axe in a death blow. Mensa evaded easily. "My Lord," he said, "I am your servant, but I am a soldier, not a dog. If you attack me again, I will be forced to defend myself. It is my right."

Shango peered at Mensa through snake eyes. "It is your right to die."

The fight was fierce and brutal. Each combatant was a skilled fighter. Shango handled his axe with ease. Mensa relied on quickness, parrying every thrust and chop. Mensa carried a short fighting spear in each hand. He was the best in the Kingdom with any weapon, but he was especially gifted with the spears.

After twenty minutes, both men were covered with sweat and blood. While neither had landed a fatal blow, they had cut each other many times. Mensa wiped blood from his face where a jagged scar showed just how close he'd come to losing his head. Shango's black blood dripped from multiple cuts on his chest, legs, and arms – vivid testimony that Mensa could have killed him but was holding back.

Shango lay his axe on the ground. "Come, little man, put down your toys and fight."

Mensa jabbed both spears, points first, into the hard ground.

The two men rushed one another. Mensa was skilled and brave, but Shango was enormous. By sheer bulk, he overcame the smaller man, flinging Mensa into the dirt close to a high cliff. As Shango approached, murder in his eyes, Mensa lunged. Shango caught him squarely in the jaw with a raised knee. Mensa staggered and collapsed.

Shango picked Mensa up and turned to hurl him over the cliff.

"My Lord, do not kill him," the Captain said from a safe distance. "If he has broken the law, he will stand trial and face discipline. We have our own ways."

Shango glared at the Captain and began to lower the unconscious Mensa. At the last moment, Shango lifted Mensa and slammed his body across his knee. The audible crack caused the men to turn their heads; several vomited.

Shango walked away. As he passed, the Captain heard him say, "Now, I take care of my treacherous wife."

CHAPTER 14

Word of the titanic fight reached Ogun almost before arrived at the palace.

"Is the guard still alive?" he asked.

"I do not know, my Lord Ogun. My spy said it sounded like your brother broke Mensa's back.

"Find him – find him and bring what is left of him to me. Now!"

When they located Mensa, he was in a coma and barely breathing. They rushed his mangled body to Ogun as fast as they could. The God of War hovered as the physician completed his examination.

"Whatever it takes, Doctor, put him back together."

"I will do my best, my Lord."

Ogun glared. "You will do better than that or there will be terrible consequences. This man is very important to me – do you understand?"

"Yes, my Lord."

Ogun turned to leave, thought better of it, and turned back. "Is he paralyzed?"

"No, my Lord. He has several broken bones, a

fractured skull, and both his lungs are collapsed. It is a miracle he is not dead."

Ogun stalked out of the room. The walls reverberated with his last command. "Make sure the miracle continues."

**

Mensa drifted in and out of consciousness over the next few days. Ogun received hourly reports – even through the night. The guards outside his bedroom listened until he finished with whatever concubine he'd selected for the evening – no one wanted to interrupt a rutting God of War – and hustled in with whatever news they had.

Mensa had a recurring dream. He stood in a meadow next to his father and grandfather. "Why are you here," Mensa asked.

"We are here to take you to your ancestral home," they replied in unison.

"I am tired," Mensa said, "But I must guard the Princess. She is still my responsibility and I feel she is in great danger."

His father spoke in a low, soothing voice. "Son, I too served the royal family in my day. I was betrayed."

"By whom, father?"

His father tried to whisper a name, but Mensa could not hear him.

As Mensa moved towards his father – every time – every night, he heard Nefertari's voice. "Mensa – Mensa – save me."

Every night, his father said, "Come with me,

son, and I will tell you the rest of the mystery. You will be home. You will be at peace."

And every night, Mensa gave the same reply, "I cannot go with you yet, Father. I must still do my duty. I must still guard the Princess."

And he would awaken, covered in sweat.

The doctor and his assistants doted over the bodyguard every minute. At Ogun's orders, the attendants fed Mensa manna – the special food of the gods. The young warrior would not have survived any other way. Made from protein and packed with nutrients and vitamins unknown to the citizens of Abzu, the spongy green substance slowly began to restore Mensa to health.

Ogun visited every day. The first few times, Mensa did not know of his presence. On the fourth day, as Ogun turned to leave, Mensa spoke, "My Lord Ogun, where am I?"

"You are in my palace."

"How did I come to be here?"

"Do you not remember?" Ogun asked, sensing an opportunity.

"The last thing I remember, Lord Shango came over the hill and confronted me."

Though he kept his face placid and grim, inside, Ogun beamed with delight.

"I have only heard second hand," he began. "But my understanding is that he heard you were the fiercest warrior in all of Abzu."

Mensa smiled weakly. "It is nice to be recognized for my hard labor."

"No," Ogun said. "He did not come to congratulate you or even to thank you for your lifelong dedication to the Princess. He was jealous of your reputation and bet one the members of his personal guard that he could and would destroy you in combat."

Mensa'a brow furrowed. "He did not come to thank me?"

"No," Ogun said. "He came to kill you – or so I heard."

**

Ogun continued to inject his verbal poison into Mensa's unsuspecting ears every day for the next two weeks. The God of War embellished the story, but never mentioned either Nefertari's pregnancy or Shango's jealous suspicions. The more Ogun talked, the more bewildered Mensa grew. Finally, the young soldier was indignant.

"I have served this kingdom my entire life," Mensa said. "And Shango attacked me to satisfy his ego?"

"And to win a substantial wager."

**

Three weeks after the Mensa's battle with Shango, Ogun visited again – this time late at night.

"How are you feeling?"

Mensa tried to stand but Ogun held out his hand. The bodyguard collapsed back into his pillows. "Thank you, my Lord. I apologize for my weakened condition. I am usually much more robust."

"I would guess you have seldom been so close to death," Ogun said.

Mensa shook his head. "I am still baffled by Lord Shango's attack. I have never thought he would be so cavalier about my service, to attack me to win a bet or to prove a point. I have done nothing but keep watch over his wife. I would give my life for the Princess.

Ogun laughed. *Now is the time,* he thought. "Apparently, you gave more than your life."

Mensa's brow furrowed in confusion. "I do not understand."

"You gave the Princess a child," Ogun said. "No one can violate the Nefertari's purity and live."

Despite his weakened condition, Mensa wobbled to his feet and stood before the great God of War. "On the souls of my grandfather and father, I have never acted in any inappropriate way with Princess Nefertari. I pledged to protect her. To me, that means her life *and* her reputation."

Ogun was given to cynicism, but something about the young man's earnest face told him Mensa was speaking the truth.

"You never touched her in a sexual way?"

"I never touched her at all other than to assist her onto her mount or to cross a stream when she was on a hike."

Ogun bit the inside of his lip for a while. The young man was earnest – and honest – two obvious character flaws. *I can use his rube,* Shango thought. *I just have to maneuver him back into my brother's good graces.*

"Leave everything to me," he said. "But whatever happened, remember one thing."

"What, my Lord?"

A sinister sneer creased Ogun's lips. "Shango is the one who tried to kill you. I am the one who saved our worthless life."

Mensa bowed as best he could.

"Yes, my Lord. I do not know how I can ever repay you."

"A time will come," Ogun said, "When you will have the opportunity to help me. I trust you will recognize it when it arises. You are a man of honor – I know you will remember the kindness I have shown."

Mensa again did obeisance despite the pain. "I hear and obey, Lord Ogun."

Ogun smiled as he left the room. *Now, I may have found my spy.*

CHAPTER 15

The rage burning within Shango had not subsided when he returned to the palace. He hurled a guard who was a little slow opening the door into a wall, which broke the unfortunate soldier's arm. Servants and courtiers scurried out of sight when they heard the great god's roar.

"Where is my wife?

He burst into their bedroom, nearly ripping the hinges off the twelve-foot doors. The crash awakened Nefertari from a deep sleep. She rubbed her eyes and smiled.

"Oh, my husband, you are back. I was worried because you left so quickly. I would have stayed awake, but the little one (she gazed down at her belly) is already making me tired. Imagine how exhausted I will be when I have to chase…"

She broke off when she looked at Shango's face – a portrait of murderous rage. Red blood – a human's – mixed with his own black stains, covering him in a macabre pattern of grisly splotches.

"Husband," she said climbing from the bed, "What is wrong?"

Shango's raised palm stopped her. "Do not approach me, whore. I cannot be responsible for what I might do. Even gods have their breaking point."

Nefertari exploded in tears. "You call me w—w-whore? What have I done?"

"We can play games all night, if you like," he said. "But you know what you have done."

The regal bearing returned and Nefertari's eyes blazed with indignation. "And what do you think I have done, husband." She spat out the last word like she'd eaten something foul.

"You bedded your bodyguard – the one called Mensa."

Shango expected tears – a denial – a show of defiance. He stepped back when Nefertari burst into laughter.

"Mensa? Mensa? The man who is like an older brother to me? Were I ever to take a lover, husband (again, spoken with distaste), I would choose someone who did not feel like a blood relative."

Shango suddenly slumped onto the floor. His head was pounding and his ears ringing with the Holy Imperatives – the rules by which he was obligated to operate.

The humans are there to serve you, but you will honor their traditions.

You shall not interfere in their tribal matters.

Never assert yourself or your power into human history.

You may take a human woman as a consort but never as a spouse.

You may never harm a human except in self-defense.

He had endured a reprimand for the wedding but killing one of the tribe members would result in his immediate demotion and recall. He could not go back – he would not go back – to that dying place with its rigid caste system and corrupt governance. He would die before he left this...this...paradise where he was a god – worshiped by men – desired by women.

And loved by Nefertari. Even in his anger, Shango knew that. But at this moment, Shango wanted nothing more than to hurt someone else – to make someone pay for the indignity he was enduring, the humiliation he would feel. The great god Shango, cuckold, fool, dupe – betrayed by his wife with a commoner.

He looked into his wife's cavernous eyes. He saw no duplicity – no trickery or deceit. Could she be telling the truth?

"If the child is not Mensa's, to whom does it belong?"

"Why you, husband. You are the only man I have been with – ever. You know I was a maiden when we married. I have never been unfaithful. Why would I trifle with silly humans when I go to bed every night with the most virile man in the world?"

While Nefertari was being honest, she also

knew Shango's weak spot – his immense ego. The minute she uttered the last sentence, she saw him swell with pride. And she saw the anger drain from him like pus from a lanced boil.

He put out his hand to touch her shoulder, but she recoiled.

"Husband," she said, "Whose blood covers your body? Do not lie – you have not been hunting. Besides, when you hunt, you always cleanse yourself before entering this room."

When Shango's head dropped, Nefertari knew the answer. She did not wait for an answer. She stood from the bed and walked out of the room.

Shango, the great God of Thunder sat on the edge of the bed and wept.

Down the hall, in a separate bedroom, Nefertari clutched her pillow. The baby within her would eventually be a great source of joy, but this evening, thoughts of the child filled her with bitterness and pain. She fell asleep with tears streaming down her face.

CHAPTER 16

The silver worm ate through the mountain like a weevil through a cotton boll. Its mighty jaws gnawed a path five cubits[6] wide and eight cubits[7] high. The earth disappeared into the dark maw, traveled the length of the beast (at least twenty cubits[8]) and reappeared from its rectum transformed into gold. The members of the Abzu tribe thought it was magic.

Shango, Ogun, and their lieutenants knew it was something else – technology.

"The mining cylinder works marvelously well, brother," Ogun said. "I am rather proud of it."

"As well you should be, brother," Shango said. "Your design as effective as it is deceptive. Just remind those inside that they can never been seen by any of the humans."

"Those ignorant beings believe it to be a – let's see – yes, a 'silver worm.'"

Shango turned and faced his smirking brother. "And the minute one of your technicians gets sloppy and exits the craft where he can be seen, one of those 'ignorant beings' will understand exactly what is going on."

"How would they ever understand that the people inside the cylinder are separating the gold from the dirt and other minerals?"

"They may be uneducated by our standards," Shango said. "But they are far from stupid. I dare say, were it not for their ingenuity, you and I might well starve here. The manna can only last so long."

"True," Ogun said, "And compared to the local dishes – especially the delicacy they call roast lamb – manna tastes like something from the back end of a goat."

"Only you would know what goat shit tastes like, brother," Shango said laughing.

Ogun laughed, but he hated the way Shango continually bettered him in a battle of wits. And he was growing increasingly bitter that in all their staged battles, Shango always won.

Things had always been this way. When Ogun was ten, his life changed forever; Shango appeared. Emperor Anu grinned from ear-to-ear as he held his new baby boy.

"This child represents a new generation of leaders," Anu said. He held the baby aloft as if showing off a championship trophy. "I will call him Shango, meaning 'The One Who Strikes.' He will be mighty, strong, and faster, but he will also be more intelligent than anyone in the Empire. I will personally train him. He will be the first of a new race – a race of super beings. When I am gone, he will lead this Empire to greater success than it has ever known."

Little did the Emperor know that Ogun was listening from behind a piece of furniture.

Ogun was only a child, but he understood the order of succession very well. He knew the mantle of leadership was supposed to be his – and his alone. When Anu died (or abdicated), the entire world was destined to bow before Emperor Ogun, the 'god of iron.' Leadership was his birthright. Now he was to be replaced by this puking, squalling lump.

No one was ever aware that Ogun knew about Anu's intentions. The old man never talked about the future with either son except in the broadest of terms. While Anu always treated Ogun with respect, when the time came for the expedition to Pangea, Anu put Shango in charge.

"Ogun, my son, you are a magnificent warrior. Your bravery is equal to, if not greater, than mine. Your brother is a brilliant scientist. His understanding of technology is rivaled only by that of Bondu – and you will overtake him in a short time. While you are skilled in the art of war, Shango has an adventurous spirit. He also needs some experience. For this mission, I have chosen him to lead."

"Will I have to take orders from him, father?"

"Any orders will come from me," Anu said. "And you will both obey my commands without equivocation. But if there are mission-critical decisions to be made and you two cannot agree, Shango will have the final say."

Ogun had swallowed both his anger and his

pride, but the resentment built steadily – and the dam was about to burst.

CHAPTER 17

Many thought Dindaka was immortal, but the pains he felt in different – and increasingly new – places every morning told him otherwise. Mensa arrived at the opening to the mines of Azbu in the dead of night accompanied by six of Ogun's most trusted bodyguards. (Like Shango, Ogun had no need of the soldiers – but all the gods were vain and liked the pomp and prestige of personal protection.) Dindaka knew everything – the Princess's pregnancy – the rumors of infidelity – the story of the beating Shango had administered to Mensa. But Dindaka also knew of Nefertari's fury with her husband and how she had threatened to leave him (and to take the expected child) if Shango ever raised his hand to Mensa again.

Shango claimed, truthfully, that he had no idea as to Mensa's location. Since his scouts had not found a body when they went to find it, the Thunder God assumed the bodyguard was either hiding in one of the innumerable caves dotting the low hills or had been eaten by one of the carnivorous beasts.

Everyone knew Shango abhorred the mines;

Dindaka's meeting with Mensa would be uninterrupted. There was no moon. It would not have mattered. The pit at the mine was so deep, it was gloomy even when the noon sun blazed. Mensa arrived early and waited, gazing at the dark sky and thinking about Nefertari, wondering if he would ever see her again.

"Hello, boy." Dindaka voice echoed against the walls of the pit.

No one had ever successfully surprised Mensa – at least not since he became a warrior. "Do not doubt your skills, my son," Dindaka said. "We of the Magi can cloak ourselves in the Deep Mysteries. Had I not spoken, I could have walked past you without your knowing."

Mensa embraced the old man. "I need help," he said.

"You wish to know if you can return to your princess without losing your life."

Mensa did not even ask how Mensa knew – the old man always knew – everything. "Yes," he said.

"And you also wonder if you can trust me," Dindaka said.

Mensa hung his head.

"Do not be ashamed, boy," Dindaka said. "You have the instincts of a cheetah. You know when you may be in danger. Your intuition will serve you well. To answer your second question, I will always tell you the truth. I am incapable of lying."

"That is true of all your people, correct?"

"Yes and no. True, we never lie. But we are not

a people – we are a select order. To become a Magi, you must be chosen. We pick and train only the brightest and the best. While we admire physical accomplishment, we are more impressed by mental dexterity. People like you who are both strong and smart are prime candidates for the Order."

"I am honored by your comments, Dindaka," Mensa said.

"Were I to lie to you, I would be cast out," Dindaka said. "If I were to be cast out, I would end my life – I could not bear the shame."

Mensa's eyes had adjusted to the dark. He could see Dindaka's lined and sincere face. There was no falsehood in the man. "Father," he said – many people called Dindaka "Father" – "can I return to the palace?"

Without hesitation, Dindaka said, "You may, and you should. The Princess needs you now more than ever."

"Trusting you, I will go at once," Mensa said.

He turned to leave. Dindaka held him in a surprisingly strong grip. "Before you go, Mensa, I need to tell you something. Though you did not ask, you deserve to know the truth."
**

Mensa had not closed his mouth for five minutes, his jaw slack in stupefied wonder.
"Do you think she knows?" he asked. "How could she hide such evil from me for so long?

Dindaka reached out and gently lifted Mensa's chin to close the guard's mouth.

"She does not know," Dindaka said. " No, the Princess is everything she appears to be. I think she is one of the loveliest creatures in Abzu – maybe anywhere. Perhaps she is too naïve to know of her brother's vile nature. I think she is simply so kind that she chooses not to believe what she has undoubtedly heard."

Silence lay on the floor like a lazy dog until Mensa chose to speak. Though hesitant, he wanted to know. Finally, Mensa slammed his palm against his forehead. "I am confused, Father," he said. "What do you think she 'undoubtedly heard?'"

Dindaka pursed his lips and began again.

"Many springs ago, before even your father was born, your grandfather was king of Abzu." He held up a finger to stop Mensa's question. "Yes, your grandmother was Queen Efia of Abzu as I suspect she has recently told you. She was a blessing to the people – far more impressed with what her power enabled to her to do for others than what she could achieve for herself. She was beloved. Your grandfather Bala was a mighty warrior, a scholar, and a man of integrity.

"When Bala was eighteen, the King died, leaving no queen and no descendants. Lord Shango had been here for a long time but refused to participate in selecting a new monarch. He said the people should pick their own leader according to the local custom, so the Elders met to choose a new king. Gamba's father, Lord Akil, asked for trial by combat. He thought the new monarch should face and kill all rivals before ascending to the throne. Akil was a fierce fighter, but he was not as skilled as your grandfather."

"Did Bala kill him?"

"No, there was no fight. Despite continual pressure from Akil and his supporters, the Elders decided to leave the decision up to the Land. They prayed for a sign. They prayed for twenty-one days. After three weeks, a fierce storm arose unlike anything anyone had ever seen. There were hailstones the size of a lion's head. Rain fell in buckets. The Zambezi dam was close to bursting. As you know, birds seldom fly in bad weather, but on the morning of the twenty-first day, three birds flew through the teeth of gale and into our village."

Mensa leaned forward.

"Your grandfather was standing in the middle of the village." Even in the dark, Dindaka's eyes blazed as he spoke. "He and the other elders were still praying for a sign, just as they had every day. Akil was there as well. The three birds all landed at the same time. And they all landed on your grandfather. Right then, the Elders knew they had their sign."

Mensa made a face. "Really? Birds? How was that a sign."

Dindaka's smile spoke of another place and another time as he remembered. "These were just not any birds," he said. "The first was a dove who landed on your grandfather's right hand – the hand with which he gripped his spear. It was a dove. The

Elders knew that meant your grandfather would bring peace to our village.

"The second bird was a hawk. It landed on his shoulder – a sign that, when needed – your grandfather would be fearless and valiant."

"What was the third?" Mensa asked with the enthusiasm of a child.

"The third was an owl," Dindaka said. "It perched atop Bala's head – the sign of wisdom. And the moment the owl alit on your grandfather's head, the rain stopped."

Mensa could not restrain himself very long. "What did Lord Akil do? He must have been angry."

"Oh," Dindaka said, "He was furious, but he was also cunning. He realized he would not win the throne – not after such a sign. So, he rushed to your grandfather and knelt before him. He shouted, 'Hail, O gracious king!' And all the Elders joined in. But the moment they coronated Bala as their next monarch, Akil began to weave his plot."

CHAPTER 18

Emperor Anu was the father of many children, most of them women. Though he regularly communicated with his two sons on Pangaea, he had never visited. Today was a special occasion.

Today, after three years, Anu was meeting Shango and Ogun in person.

Over six and a half cubits tall[9] and muscular, Anu struck an imposing figure in his custom-tailored military uniform. He preferred this style of dress to more casual clothing. He felt – correctly – that is radiated power.

Anu was Master of the Realm, Sovereign of the Universe, and Commander-in-Chief of the Supreme Galactic Force. At his word, destruction would rain on any land, nation, or leader who so much as questioned his decisions. He loved his sons, but he expected absolutely loyalty and obedience.

The High Council had expressed concerns about the Pangaea operation. Gold production was lower than required. The precious metal originally made up just over one quarter of the atmosphere of the Home Planet. Its supplies were dwindling at an alarming rate. Only those in power could afford to have the naturally pulverized element pumped into their palaces. The poorer citizens (who could not purchase over-priced filter masks) slowly fell into ill health – and died.

Every death meant one less person using up precious, microscopic bits of gold.

The expedition to Pangaea had originally been intended to determine if residents of Nauru could adapt to a nitrogen/oxygen atmosphere. Shango and Ogun had not only adapted but had also flourished. They took almost no time to adjust to the new air – in fact, they had grown stronger. While both of them still required occasional injections of gold, their consumption lessened every month. Soon, they would be free of the nuisance.

Even though the Emperor's sons had taken to life on Pangaea like ducks to water, the High Council had changed the nature of their mission when gold was discovered in mass quantities. Much of it lay on the ground in nuggets the size of walnuts. The natives liked the shiny color but attached no value to the metal because it was so commonplace. At the Council's insistence, a team of geologists had landed on Pangaea to conduct field tests and exploration. Within two days, they had discovered the hill country in the Kingdom of Abzu was riddled with massive veins of gold.

The directive came to Shango and Ogun. "Put the natives to work. Mine the gold. Ship it home. Once we have depleted the deposit, destroy all evidence of your trip – and dispose of the indigenous population." That had been almost two hundred Earth years ago.

The population has resisted at the beginning. Abzu was an advanced civilization that lived in cooperation with the *surface* of the Earth. They did not consider savaging The Mother for what lay *underneath*. Abzubians worked hard – labor did not frighten them, but they did not understand the god's fascination – no, obsession – with the soft, yellow substance called "gold."

Still, Shango insisted and they people felt they must, out of obedience to the deity, do as he requested. Lord Ogun was less gentle – or so they heard. News traveled fast in Pangea. When Ogun forced the Eleekans to work from dawn to dusk, the good folks in Abzu heard. When Eleekans were beaten for putting a shiny nugget in their pouches (children loved to watch the sun glint from the mineral), Abzu heard. When Ogun took wives and daughters and made them do unspeakable things while their men were in the mines, Abzu seethed.

But Lord Shango was gentle and kind. While he set quotas, when they were not met, he held conferences with the Elders to determine if the goals were realistic. If they were not, they were changed. If they were, the group devised incentive plans to excite the miners. The mining operation had been in place for generations. Miners in Abzu worked only four hours a day now, thanks to "the Worm."

At first, assisted by Shango's ingenious mining craft – a silver cylinder secretly housing six scientists who manipulated mineralogical equipment designed to separate gold from other elements – production soared. The natives called it "The Worm" and simply trundled behind the craft collecting the gold as it spewed from the ejection port at the rear. While they still could not understand the fascination with a worm's excrement, Shango and Ogun commanded it. The Elders said, "It is important to the gods. Ours is not the place to question their wisdom."

The operation was a complete success. Shango's geologists estimated they could completely tap all the ore-rich veins in four to five Nauruian[10] years. But there was a fly in the ointment.

Because of their enormous size, marvelous technology, and advanced fighting skills, Shango and Ogun had been mistaken for divine creatures the minute they arrived in Pangea. "They do what only gods can."

The people brought tokens of affection meant to curry favor. The brothers accumulated vast stores of earthly riches. More to their liking, the natives thought nothing of offering the most beautiful of their nubile virgins (or experienced concubines depending on the brothers' mood) for Shango and Ogun's carnal enjoyment. The women of Nauru, rendered incapable of natural reproduction, had largely lost interest in sex eons before.

They might consent to a coupling on a wedding night or some special anniversary, but life in Nauru was largely asexual. Once Shango and Ogun were introduced to regular sexual dalliances, it was not unusual for either brother to "partake" of the attentions of a half-dozen women in the course of one evening.

One day, Ogun had spoken to Shango. "My brother, it is a shame the mining machine has developed some technical issues."

Shango, a scientist and inventor, was aghast. "What do you mean, brother? I will attend to it at once."

Ogun, suspecting all their conversations were monitored, winked at this brother.

"I am sure you will do your best, brother," he said. "But the problems seem particularly nettlesome. It appears production will be slowed, and we will be forced to stay in the mudhole for some indeterminable amount of time."

Shango caught on and nodded in understanding. "Yes, brother. That is a pity. But I pledge I will do everything in my power to get production back up to maximum levels."

Shango worked on the machine as promised, by himself. He installed newly-designed and virtually undetectable features that limited the machine's processing ability. Ever cautious about informants, Shango never discussed the modifications with anyone. But his brother completely understood when Shango said, "Ogun, I have done everything I can. The mining will continue, but I am afraid maximum production will be limited to fifty pounds a day."

Ogun smiled and in a rare display of affection, kissed his younger brother on the cheek.

CHAPTER 19

Dindaka continued with his tale.

"Bala's rule was spectacular. The nation thrived. Because of his great reputation as a warrior and general, no other nation trifled with Abzu. Chieftains came from all over Pangea to pay tribute to the mighty Bala. They brought gifts and riches. But Bala was so magnanimous, every visitor left richer than he came."

"Why would grandfather not just accept the tribute? He would have been very wealthy?"

Dindaka placed a long index finger next to his temple. "Your grandfather was very smart. He was not interested in the riches of the world but in the betterment of the world. He knew widespread peace was more important and lasting than personal wealth."

He moved his finger to his chest. "Besides, Bala was already a rich man. He had the biggest heart in the world."

Inexplicably, Mensa felt a tear run down his cheek. He looked away momentarily to brush it.

"Do not be ashamed, my boy," Dindaka said.

"Only a real man can show his emotions. Why do you weep? Are you sad you did not inherit wealth beyond measure?"

"That is not it, Father."

"No, you weep with pride – pride in the inheritance you have – your heart, your courage and, most importantly – your character."

"What happened to my grandfather? I am very confused. I was always told he was a bodyguard."

"Pfft." Dindaka spat. "He was nothing of the sort." Sensing he might have wounded Mensa, he said, "There is nothing wrong with the calling, my boy. You are a man of bravery and of honor – as was Bala. It's just that the bodyguard story was constructed especially for you – more precisely for your father, Jandal."

Mensa peered through the gloom. "What do you mean?"

Dindaka drew circles in the dust with his cane. "Bala was the king – Efia was the queen. They had not been able to have children. Everyone knew the crown would fall to Akil. After all, he might have been king had it not been for the sign of the birds.

"Logical," Mensa said.

"Though Akil hated serving your grandfather, he knew his time was coming. He was younger – Bala had to die some time. Then, Akil would assume the throne. But something happened – something joyful for the Kingdom – something tragic for Akil."

"What was that?"

"Efia announced she was with child – she would give birth to your father. The House of Mensa would retain the crown."

"So, Akil killed Bala?"

Dindaka raised his head and studied the distant night sky. A lone star was the only thing dispelling the black velvet curtain.

"It is a serious thing to charge someone with murder," Dindaka said. "It is even more serious to say they committed regicide. No one ever uttered the word aloud, but there have always been whispers. And I am convinced of Akil guilt."

"What happened."

"To celebrate Jandal's birth, Bala declared a hunt. It was more of a party, but it gave the men of the Kingdom a change to gather – along with the women who wished to join. As you know, Abzu prides itself on its female warriors."

Mensa nodded and smiled as he remember Nefertari and her considerable outdoor skills.

Dindaka's voice grew softer. "They had been gone only two days – the hunt was scheduled for a week. When they returned so soon, everyone knew there had been a problem. Your grandfather, the King of Abzu, had been gored by the Royal Elephant."

"The one on which he rode?" Mensa's face registered confusion. "All kings ride a beast that is meticulously trained, loyal, and docile."

"Yes," Mensa said. "But Akil claimed to have witnessed the event with his men. He said that he was with Bala and the Royal Guards. According to his story, Bala was on foot, which mean he had dismounted. Pom-Pom, the Royal Elephant, was gentle and exquisitely trained. Those who were in other places heard shouting and returned to find all six members of the Royal Guard dead. Pom-Pom was dying. Akil claimed a tiger had attacked and that the soldiers had accidentally stabbed and slashed Pom-Pom while trying to kill the cat."

"Did Bala have the same story?"

"No one will ever know," Dindaka said. "He was dead – impaled on Pom-Pom's tusk. Akil claimed the elephant was thrashing around and buried his tusk into the King."

Mensa shook his head. "Surely, it that were not true, one of the other witnesses would have said so."

Dindaka patted Mensa on the knee. "Boy, do you find it odd that the only men killed by either tiger or elephant were the King and his men. None of Akil's men had so much as a hangnail."

"Well," Mensa said, "Strange things happen on a hunt."

"True," Dindaka said. "But stranger still is that within two weeks, every one of Akil's men who had been at the scene died or disappeared. There were, of course, explanations, but a few of us on the Council of Elders saw through the ruse. Those who spoke up were executed for treason."

Mensa scowled. "You have always been known as a man of honor, Dindaka. Why did you remain silent?"

The old man paused for a long time. When he finally spoke, his voice was a whisper. "Because of your father, dear boy. Because of your father."

CHAPTER 20

Neither Shango nor Ogun knew anything about the imperial visit ahead of time. Anu's arrival was announced after his craft landed. The brothers met at the door of the ship, not a run-about "dragon," but a massive, interplanetary dreadnaught capable of light speed travel. With an advanced fuel system, its cruising radius was virtually limitless. As soon as it had landed, a sophisticated stealth system engaged, and the craft became indistinguishable from its surroundings. Shango and Ogun could only locate it via the coordinates the Emperor had sent to them.

"Why are we here?" Shango asked.

"I do not know," Ogun replied. "But to my knowledge, father has not left Nauru since the days of the Great War on the Blue Planet."

Shango shook his head. "This cannot be good."

The Emperor greeted his sons with formal courtesy. When his attendants left the room, he embraced them both. They exchanged pleasantries and information from "back home." Anu motioned for his sons to sit.

"I am here because of a complaint," he said.

"Of what nature?" Shango said. "Surely this could have been handled without the trouble of your personal visit."

"The complaint concerns you directly, my son," Anu. "And your marriage to the woman of Abzu."

"I have sent my apologies to the High Council, Father. I believe that is sufficient."

Rage furrowed Shango's brow. "Father, you know the ban on marriage to the humans is only to prevent the outbreak of war."

The Emperor nodded. "Yes, we learned the hard way because of the unfortunate incident with Ogun and Ife."

Ogun visible flinched but said nothing.

The Emperor stroked his chin. "There is the matter of the impending child."

Shango was not disturbed. "Surely, Father, you knew about this as soon as I did. You know all things almost as they happen. Your network of informants is unmatched."

"Yes, my son," Anu said. "And I am not happy, but I was willing to let the indiscretion pass until the entire Council learned of the pregnancy. As I said, there was a complaint."

Shango stood in amazement. "Someone filed a charge? Who was it?"

The voice next to him sounded. "It was me, brother," Ogun said. "I filed it."

Shango's first instinct was to seize his

brother by the throat. His father intervened. "Do not dare touch Ogun," he said. "He simply followed protocol."

Ogun knew he'd been saved a beating, but the Emperor would not be there forever. He scrambled to make amends.

"You are too involved, my brother. It is fine to fornicate with the women here – they are willing, beautiful, and some of them are quite accomplished. But this is becoming dangerous."

Shango was about to speak to his brother when a thought hit him.

"Father, I have suspected Nefertari of infidelity. Because of my great love for her, I have put my anger aside and will raise the child as my own. If my wife slept with another man, you might be upset, but you would not interfere. You would not be here unless you *knew* I was the father of this baby."

Anu slumped into a seat, the only time either son had seen anything close to weakness from their all-powerful father.

**

No one spoke for close to fifteen minutes. The Emperor stared at the wall. He was coming to a decision. Shango and Ogun knew better than to disturb his meditations. When he eventually looked at his sons, his eyes were rimmed with tears.

"My sons," he said, "You had another brother."

Shango and Ogun looked at one another, then back to their father.

"His name was Marvex. He was a brilliant scientist. Unfortunately, he was also great warrior and a commander in the Imperial Army. While serving his mandatory military service as Governor of the Blue Planet, civil war broke out. He was betrayed by a duplicitous cabinet minister who came up from behind and stabbed him with a poison-encrusted dagger. Loyal members of his cabinet rushed him home for medical attention, but we could not save him.

"On the day he died, I secretly extracted some of his Life Matter[11]. I saved it for many years – decades – until we discovered this seemingly insignificant universe and sent an exploratory party to this planet. The first expedition brought back trophies from this place – animals, minerals – and a woman. She was wild and savage, but strong. It took years for me to gain her trust."

Ogun looked at his father. "Did you take her, father?"

"Don't be common, Ogun," the Emperor said. "By that time in my life, I was above such trivial matters. I did not, as you so crudely put it, 'take her,' but I did convince her to bear a child. Using a secret technique I developed myself, I combined her Life Force with what I had harvested from your brother. The result (here he turned to Shango) was you, my son."

Shango sat in stunned silence turning the matter over in his mind.

"Then you are not my father," he said. "Technically, you are my grandfather and my brother is my father."

"Biologically, yes," Anu said. "But I have loved you for your entire life like my son and treated you that way."

Ogun erupted. "You have treated this *bastard* better than your son," he said. "You have always favored him over me."

The roar came from deep inside the Emperor, "Silence!"

The room fell still. "I love both of you deeply," he said. "Each of you has gifts. But you, Shango, are unique among all our people. You were never sterilized. Unlike any other man from our planet, you can spread your seed, and repopulate our race throughout the Universe. You are our hope!"

CHAPTER 21

"What did Jandal have to do with your silence, Father?" Mensa could feel the hair on the back of his head standing. "I have admired you all my life. You let my grandfather's death go unpunished and now you blame it on my father?

He brushed Dindaka's hand away. The old man replaced it and patted the knee again.

"You are smart, Mensa," he said. "You are skilled. But you are not always wise. Sometimes you have to look at the bigger picture. Your father was less than two weeks old. Even in our wonderful nation, newborns die at a startling rate. After a state funeral, the Council met and named Akil regent – he was to rule until your father reached his age of majority. Immediately upon his appointment, Akil moved into the palace. He found Efia busily directing the staff to pack up and leave."

"Why would she do that?"

"Your grandmother said it was to allow Akil the freedom to rule until Jandal was of age. But she suspected foul play and wanted to get as far away as possible."

"What happened?"

"Akil appointed a personal guard of four men for Prince Jandal. He was never out of their sight."

Mensa put his hand atop Dindaka's. "They were assigned to kill him if..."

Dindaka interrupted. "If Efia offered the least resistance or if anyone – including me – ever suggested that he had murdered the King. I suspected – in my heart, I know. But since I did not have proof and all the witnesses to the crime were gone, I determined the wise course of action was to stay silent and do everything I could to protect you."

Neither man spoke for a while. Though it remained dark, the retreating shadows signaled the approach of dawn.

"What sort of man was my father?"

"The finest I have ever known. He was fierce in life – all of it. He attacked everything. He knew he would be king. He trained for it every day. He ran to strengthen his body. He debated every issue with anyone who would listen – me usually or another Magi – to build his mind. He loved to solve riddles. No one could stump him. He was the best spear fighter and the finest archer in all the land. When he hunted, while the other hid away and attacked beasts from secret locations, your father stood on the plain and waited until he saw a boar or a leopard or a rogue elephant. Then, he would chase it down and do battle one-on-one."

"He always won."

"Always. Right up until his last expedition."

"When was that?"

"Two days before his eighteenth birthday on the last hunt before he was to assume the throne."

"Did Akil go on the hunt?"

"Yes."

Mensa's jaw clenched. "All this time, I have been told my father died protecting the Royal Family. Let me guess. He was gored by an elephant."

"No, my son," Dindaka said with a hint of an ironic grin. "No one would have believed that tale. This time, it was a wild boar. The details differed slightly, but the story was essentially the same."

Mensa's voice quavered with rage. "Akil should have paid for his crimes."

Now, Dindaka laughed aloud – this deep chuckle echoing into nothingness down the mine shaft. "In way, he did."

Mensa was pacing. "What do you mean?"

"Many years later, Akil was himself killed while on a hunting trip. This time, the culprit was a leopard. I was on the hunt and rushed to the King's side when I heard the blast from the horn. I took one look at the scene and knew it had been staged."

"How?"

"Three things," Dindaka said. "First, all the King's personal guards were dead – just as your grandfather's had been. Second, the offending leopard, although dead, could not have killed a mouse. It was old and almost toothless. I know – I looked. But the third reason was the most telling."

Mensa seized Dindaka by the shoulders.

"What was it?"

"There was only one survivor to the 'vicious attack' – one witness to tell the tale."

"Who was it?"

"The only person left alive was the very man who placed you in the Imperial Guard where he could keep an eye on you – Akil's nineteen-year-old son, Gamba."

CHAPTER 22

The brazier crashed against the wall. Servants rushed to smother the burning coals before they set the palace ablaze.

"He did not even reprimand him," Ogun said in a voice loud enough to have been heard in the valley. "Shango defies every Council edict, marries a human, impregnates her, nearly kills her suspected lover, and Father tells him he is "our hope!" He flung a hand-crafted vase the entire length of the throne room. The priceless gift from the King of Nubia exploded in thousands of slivers. "The hope! Shango, the God of Thunder, a bastard child of the test tube – the Hope!"

The servants cringed in anticipation of another launch, but Ogun slumped onto his throne and stared into space. The God of War mumbled to himself. "He is no brother of mine. He is not fit to rule."

The longer Ogun sat, the angrier he grew. He remembered every lesson Anu had taught him, every time his father had issued a reproof or punishment. In Ogun's mind, he'd been rebuked for even the smallest indiscretion while Shango got away with everything. Decades of resentment boiled over, and Ogun came to a decision.

"Summon my War Council," he said. "The days of Shango's rule – no, the days of Shango's life – are over."

***

Woman on Pangea had been giving birth longer than anyone could remember. But no human had ever given birth to the child of a god. The first labor pain caused Nefertari to gasp; the second knocked her to her knees. For the first time ever, Mensa touched the Princess without first asking permission. He swept her into his arms and carried her to her room where he placed her gently on the bed.

Naomi was right behind him. "Get away from her, silly man," she said as she began arranging pillows and issuing instructions to a legion of fan bearers. Addressing Mensa again, she said, "Get out – all the way out. And do not come in here no matter what you hear. Do I make myself clear?"

Mensa had never heard the greatest general speak with such a commanding tone. "Yes," he said. Then again, "Yes," in case she had misunderstood.

Within minutes of his closing the door, Shango appeared next to him. The two men nodded to one another. Neither spoke.

Mensa did not know that Shango had instructed the servants to feed manna to Nefertari. Neither man knew the substance, well-respected by Shango and Ogun as restorative, gifted Nefertari with limited telepathic abilities. She could "talk" with her unborn child and she could sometimes hear the thoughts of others.

Several hours after the ordeal began, King Gamba joined Mensa and Shango as they paced. The trio walked in a long oval down one side of the hall, then back on the other. They spaced themselves several arms'-length apart, thus relieving them of the burden of communication.

At twilight, a servant rushed down the hall and bowed. "My Lord Shango," he said. "Emissaries from the nation of Tonga have arrived and request your immediate presence."

"Tell them to be gone" Shango said. But Gamba raised a hand.

"Hold," he said. He turned to Shango. "My Lord, I realize you are consumed with concern from your wife – my beloved sister. The throne room is but a minute of so from here. You know we have been negotiating with Tonga for some time, seeking their permission to mine gold in the disputed territory between our nations. While the situation with your wife is important, you have no reason to believe it is dire. Meanwhile, this may be the only time those savages from Tonga agree to come to speak with you. It would be an enormous mistake to let this opportunity pass."

Shango put a finger to his lips in thought.

Gamba continued. "We will stand guard here and let you know the minute anything changes – or if the baby arrives. Why stand her idle when you could be securing more gold and expanding the nation's influence?"

For the first time all evening, Shango spoke to Mensa. "I have issues with you, as you know. But I know you would never let anything happen to the Princess. You will not leave this post until I return?"

Mensa stood at attention. "I will never leave my post – ever, my Lord."

"Very well," Shango said.

And he walked down the hall.

**

I will stab the Princess while my companions dispatch the rest.

Nefertari heard the assassin before she saw him. Had she not eaten manna, she would have been dead – along with Naomi, the fan bearers, and the seven other handmaids, all of whom dozed from the exhaustion of the day. When the latest contraction had subsided, Nefertari had fallen asleep. She knew the next pain would come and rouse her. She always knew she needed as much rest as she could get; delivering a god-child would require significant stamina.

Only later did Nefertari realize she had read the killer's thoughts. She heard *I will stab the Princess* as clear as a bell. She bolted upright in bed, wide awake, as the razor-edged dagger descended. Instinctively, she parried the thrust with her arm and followed the defensive move with a palm strike to the attacker's nose. The startled man reeled in pain and disbelief, stumbled backward, and struck a brass water basin as he fell.

Suddenly light flooded the room – and with the light came Mensa, his twin spears drawn. He slashed two throats and impaled a third man almost before anyone blinked. The fourth assassin recovered from his fall and raced for the window. Mensa darted after him. With only a stride left between them, Mensa heard Nefertari shout. He hesitated, unsure if she was injured or had returned to the birthing process. His momentary pause allowed the killer to leap from the window and disappear into the night.

Mensa thought briefly about pursuit but heard a gurgling moan. Expecting to see a wounded Nefertari, he whirled in terror.

Naomi lay on the floor near the window. Her hands covered her side; blood seeped between her fingers. The look on her face was one Mensa had seen countless times – the look of impending death.

Nefertari opened her mouth to speak but before she could issue commands, Mensa was administering aid. Without thinking he snatched the sheet from off the royal bed and used it to apply pressure to the wound. Naomi groaned.

"Take care of the Princess," she said.

"You will be fine," Mensa said. "One of my men is bringing the doctor."

"He will be too late," Naomi said.

Mensa felt a tear trickle down his face. He had known Naomi many years – they were close friends.

"I need to tell you something," the girl said. Her voice was failing. Mensa leaned close. He pressed his ear close to her lips.

"Mensa," she said. "I have always loved you."

And she was gone.

**

Six hours later, the exhausted assassin collapsed in a heap on a marble floor.

"We failed," he said.

"I told you what the penalty would be."

"Yes."

As Ogun turned his back, he said, "Feed him to the lions."

CHAPTER 23

The baby came early in the morning. The labor had been intense, longer than any the midwife had ever seen. She looked at Nefertari, "It is as if your baby does not wish to enter the world," she said.

That's because he is a completely different child, Nefertari thought. She knew it was a boy – she had been reading his thoughts for some time. *He is the son of a god and the son of a princess. No child has such bloodlines – no child will ever have such strength.*

By contrast, the birth was easy. When the midwife told Nefertari to push, the baby entered the world spewing and fussing.

A boy – quickly name Rala, Crown Prince of Abzu.

Shango strutted through the palace as if he were the only man ever to sire a child. Whenever he entered a room, the people applauded. He appeared on the balcony outside the royal bedroom. An assembled crowd of several thousand cheered. "Shango – Rala – Shango – Rala – Shango – Rala!"

While Nefertari had recovered quickly, her heart was too heavy for public appearances.

"I have lost my sister," she said to Mensa while Shango soaked in the adoration of the mob. "The two people I know best in the world are you and her. Now, she is gone." Her eyes flooded. "Promise me you will never let anything happen to you, my dear Mensa."

"I am ever careful, your Highness," Mensa said, ever aware of her royal station and his lowly social status.

"Mensa!" Nefertari's voice was sharp. "This is not a time for formality. I am serious. If any mishap were to befall you, I would be devastated. And do not speak to me as if we have just met."

Mensa nodded in obedience. "Yes, Nefertari," he said. "I will be careful. But please remember how I must conduct myself when others are present." He gave a quick nod toward the balcony. The cheering continued: "Shango – Rala – Shango – Rala!"

"My husband is a dear man and I love him," Nefertari said. "But only two people in the world will ever completely understand me. And now one of them is gone. I know you are a soldier, but I want you to be careful."

"I will," Mensa said. "I promise."

**

Shango's voice was quiet and deadly. "What do you know of the assassins?" he asked.

General Kambon shook his head. "My Lord, the weapons, the armor, the sandals, all were non-descript. No symbols – no tribal patterns. None of them wore sandals. We cannot trace them by their footwear."

"Unfortunate," Shango said.

"But," Kambon said, "The emissaries from Tonga were more likely here to distract you. I believe the killers were from Tonga – or were at least hired by the monarch of that kingdom."

Shango paced. "The representatives who were here did not seem very interested in coming to any agreement about the mining proposal I had made."

"Precisely," Kambon said. "I believe they were stalling for time."

"I am disappointed in you, General," Shango said. "You are getting sloppy in your old age."

"Excuse me, my Lord? What did I do?"

"It's what you did not do. Did you examine the bodies of the dead assassins?"

Kambon shook his head again. "No, my Lord. Once I received the report from my captains, I gave instructions for the bodies to be burned."

The General expected an explosion. To his surprise, Shango laughed. "That is why you are a soldier and not a king, my good Kambon," Shango said. "When I arrived on the scene, I looked at each body – once. Two of them were unremarkable – nothing to be learned. But the third one was quite telling."

"In what way, my Lord?"

"The third man had the mark of an elite fighting unit under his right arm. It had been altered in an attempt at disguise, but under careful examination, the tattoo was unmistakable."

"What was it, my Lord."

"The assassin was marked with the sign of the shield and star."

"A six-pointed burst within a shield."

Kambon gasped. "That means…"

"Yes, General. That means the quartet of killers were most assuredly from Tonga. Whoever sent them did not take the precaution to eradicate the symbol. I have no doubt. The good King of Tonga tried to kill my wife and unborn child."

Kambon snapped to attention. "What are your orders?"

"Begin preparations for war."

CHAPTER 24

Mensa stood at attention before Ogun.

"My Lord," he said.

"Mensa, I am pleased to see you. You look much better than when you left here."

"All gratitude to you, my Lord," Mensa said. "Had you not saved me, I would have been some wolf's long-forgotten dinner by now."

Ogun studied the soldier's face. *This young man has no mask,* he thought. *Everything he thinks and feels is on his face. My, these humans are simple creatures – simple and stupid.*

"Why are you here, Mensa?"

"Lord Ogun, when you sent me back to Abzu, you gave no specific instruction. You simply asked that I remember your kindness and to render any assistance to you if I could."

Ogun internally patted himself on the back. *The simpleton does not realize I healed him to turn him into a spy. He merely thinks he is returning a kindness.*

"So what had brought you back to Eleeka, Mensa?"

"Lord Ogun, by now you have heard of the attempt on Princess Nefertari's life."

"A disgrace," Ogun said. "I trust everyone involved has been dealt with."

Mensa bobbed his head. "Three assassins were killed on the scene. The others fled but I am confident they will be brought to justice."

"What makes you so sure?"

"The killers were stealthy but not cunning," Mensa said. "Apparently they thought they would strike and evaporate like the mist. It never occurred to them they might be caught or killed."

"Go on."

"They were all obviously from Tonga," Mensa said. "Their garb and weapons were unremarkable. They wore no sandals. As you know, Lord Ogun, every tribe has very specific sandals."

Ogun smiled. "I have been here a while, Mensa. I am aware but thank you for reminding me. If they did not wear Tonganese clothing, how do you know where they were from?"

"One carried a tattoo under his arm," Mensa said. "It was the Tonganese crest – a star within a shield."

"Very sloppy," Ogun said. "Very sloppy indeed. They must pay the price. I will send messengers to my brother and offer to help track the remaining killer." He paused for a moment. "Mensa," he said, "You have been of great service. Stay the evening and you may have your choice of any three of the royal consorts. They are yours for the evening."

Ogun was sure the young man blushed. *What*

a rube, he thought.

"No, thank you, my Lord," Mensa said. "I must get back to my duties. I am supposed to be away on training but if I stay the night, I will be missed. I do not want to be as unwise as the assassins."

"Very good point," Ogun said. "Well then, name a reward."

"I ask for nothing other than to remain in your good favor, my Lord Ogun."

You are an idiot, Mensa. I will have you killed before long – you should have at least taken me up on the offer of a night of passion.

"So it will be," Ogun said. "Have you eaten?"

"I have not, my Lord. And I have little time."

"You are in luck," Ogun said. "We had succulent lamb earlier in the evening." He turned to an attendant. "Have a meal prepared for this brave young man – lamb, bread, fruit, and wine." He looked at Mensa who shook his head. "Make that water. It must be done quickly but with excellence. Only the best for our good friend."

As Mensa turned to leave, Ogun said, "Come back whenever you feel it is – ah – propitious for me to know something."

"I hear and obey," Mensa said. And he left.
**

Shango towered above a kneeling Mensa. "You have tested me once, soldier and almost paid for it with your life. Tell me why I should not have you punished."

Mensa remained on his knees, not as a beggar

but out of respect. He would not plead – and he was not afraid.

"I did only what I thought best for the Kingdom, Lord Shango."

"You went to Ogun without my permission or instruction. You know that is forbidden."

"Yes, Lord."

"What did you tell him?"

"That the assassins were from Tonga."

Dindaka, who had been summoned for the meeting, interrupted. "Surely, Lord Shango, Mensa was upset and looking to rally support for you and the Princess. I am sure he meant no harm. I respectfully…"

Dindaka trailed off when Shango exploded. "Silence! You are not his father, old man. What he told Ogun does not trouble me as much as the fact that he was willing to tell him anything. I have been suspicious of Mensa since he returned from his… time of recovery in Eleeka – concerned Lord Ogun might have convinced him to spy on my kingdom. Mensa claims he came back out of duty for Nefertari. I do believe he had ulterior motives – to undermine my rule and perhaps even to steal my wife."

Mensa stood. He had not been instructed to get on his feet. He had not asked permission. He stood anyway and faced Shango.

"My Lord," he said. "This is the second time you have questioned my loyalty to Abzu and my integrity. I will not allow you to do it a third time especially when you do not know what you are talking about."

An audible gasp resonated across the throne room. No one had ever challenged Shango in such a manner. Again, Dindaka stepped forward to intercede for Mensa, but Shango held up his hand and approached the young warrior.

"Speak, Mensa. Speak fast. My patience is at an end. Speak and explain to me what it is I do not know. Speak – and then I may well kill you where you stand."

Mensa never took his eyes off Shango. He stared unflinchingly at the God of Thunder and spoke in a quiet, even voice. "You know nothing of my loyalty. You know nothing of my devotion. And you know nothing of the plot to murder the Princess."

The silence was so thick it threatened to choke everyone in the room. Finally, Shango spoke, his voice not quite as cocksure as usual. "The first two issues may remain up for debate. But I am certain the assassins were Tonganese. The tattoo proves it."

"It proves nothing, my Lord, except that you were intentionally fooled."

"Fooled by whom?" Shango now stood six inches from Mensa, towering over the soldier. Mensa refused to lose eye contact.

"You were fooled by the man who engineered the plot to kill Nefertari."

"Who was that?"

Mensa voice rang with confidence and clar-

ity. "The assassins were not from Tonga. They were from the country on the other side of Abzu. They came from Eleeka and were sent by your brother, the Lord Ogun."
**

Mensa held the paper in front of Shango. "The Eleekan elite wear the sign of crossed spears. It is a simple design." He drew it.

"I am well aware of the design," Shango said.

"What is the mark of the warriors in Tonga?"

Shango huffed in frustration. "This is not school, Mensa. I do not have to answer questions."

Dindaka held up a long finger. He was beginning to understand. "Bear with him, my Lord."

"The star in the shield – they wear the sign of the star in the shield," Shango said in frustration.

"Like this," Mensa said drawing again.

"All you have to do is add a few lines and a shield," Mensa said. "It probably took less than an afternoon." He looked up – eager to see the reaction.

Shango huffed. "It proves nothing. If that is all you have, I am ready to pronounce your punishment."

"You may punish me any time you wish, Lord Shango, but I am not finished."

"Go on," Shango said, clearly irritated.

"When I told Lord Ogun that three of the assassins had been killed, he was pleased."

"As he should have been. Humans cannot be allowed to attack the gods or their families," Shango said.

"But," Mensa said, "He was especially pleased when I mentioned the Tonganese tattoo. He seemed very interested and very surprised, but he made a mistake."

"How is that?"

"I told him three had been killed and the others had escaped."

"So," Shango's finger started to fidget on his sword.

"Lord Ogun said he would contact you and – I believe his exact words were 'offer to help track the remaining killer.'"

Shango shrugged. "I don't see your point."

"Lord Shango," Mensa said. "I never said how many escaped. In fact, I intentionally said 'the others escaped.' The only way Lord Ogun would know there was only one remained assassin was if he had sent them."

CHAPTER 25

As soon as Ogun's spies relayed Shango's rage, the God of War had called General Tyreek.

"Assemble the armies. We go to war."

"With whom, my Lord? Have the Tonganese invaded?"

Another vase met its doom and exploded near the General's ear. "Abzu, you fool!" Ogun's voice sounded like a wounded and enraged tiger. "Shango saw through your idiotic plan and is preparing to attack.

Tyreek knew better than to correct Ogun, but the General thought, *But it was your idiotic plan, my Lord. I told you it was best to leave things alone."* But, he said, "I hear and obey, Lord Ogun."

Ogun's forces significantly outnumbered Shango's by almost 200,000 men. Calling Tyreek to his side, Ogun gave the order to attack.

"But they hold the high ground, my Lord. Should we not attempt a flanking maneuver or at least wait for them to come to us?"

"We will look like cowards if we wait. Besides, they have attacked us."

A foolish captain spoke. "Lord Ogun, technically, we have invaded them. We crossed over the boundary several furlongs[12] back."

It was the last time the captain opened his mouth. Ogun broke his jaw with a vicious backhand.

"You have your orders, General," Ogun said.

The Eleekan troops marched forward beating their spears against their shields. It was a fearsome sight. Each man wore a shining, plumed helmet and carried a shield of red leather. They marched in precise step – the line never wavered. Other armies might have charged but it was the Eleekan custom to approach at a march – a reminder of the unavoidable and unrelenting approach of death.

The Abzubians held firm, each man and woman prepared to fulfill the soldier's pledge: "I will serve my kingdom with all my skill until I can serve no more." The twin battle lines smeared into one another and the battle commenced. Though combatants fought and fell, neither side relented, and the front remained in place for three days.

As was the custom, hostilities ended precisely when the sun began to dip into the western sky. There was no signal – no flag – no horn. The soldiers just knew. They disengaged, saluted one another, and withdrew to their respective camps knowing the confrontation would renew in the morning.

General Kambon and Mensa watched from

their vantage point next to Shango. Mensa begged to fight, but Shango would not permit it. "I need your mind, Mensa," he said. "You are the finest tactician in all of Abzu – no offense to you, General Kambon."

The General bowed. "None taken, Lord Shango. I take it as a compliment. I trained Mensa myself. His understanding of the battlefield far exceeds mine and I am proud."

Still, Mensa chaffed.

At dawn of the third day, the Eleekans began their rhythmic approach again.

And everything changed.

**

Everyone could hear the whine – a screeching cacophony that grew closer by the second. When the Eleekan line was about a furlong from the Abzubians, it parted, and the creatures bolted forward as if propelled by lightning.

"It is the leopards," Mensa said. "Lord Ogun has broken the sacred law."

The Leopard Division's ferocity was the stuff of legend. Every member of the select Eleekan unit wore a headdress fashioned from a leopard's head – each man's mouth showed between two rows of open fangs. The soldiers devoted themselves exclusively to the life of a warrior – they abstained from sex, ate only raw meat, drank only spring water, and trained relentlessly. Their ferocity and skill were unmatched.

But the most unique feature was that each soldier, upon induction into the unit, was presented with a leopard cub that he (only men were allowed in the division) raised and trained. The animals were beautiful and – here was the point of Mensa's outrage – purely ceremonial.

From a time long before the gods arrived, all people of Pangea knew the Ancient Law that applied to the beasts of the Earth: "They will not suffer for our evil." The inhabitants of Pangea never hunted animals for sport – only for food – they never staged fights between the beasts ("Can a bear defeat a tiger") and they were forbidden from involving the creatures of the forest if war erupted. The innocent animals were never supposed to suffer because nations could not live in peace.

As the leopards broke into the open, the Eleekan archers fired special arrows at their enemy. Each arrow was tipped with a pouch of bull's blood. When the arrows struck, blood splattered everywhere. The leopards, deprived of food for three days and intentionally agitated (on Ogun's direct orders) could not help themselves. When they smelled the fresh blood, their instincts took over and they dove into the Abzubians in a teeth-bared search for something to eat!

The rigidly-trained, unflinchingly brave Abzu fighters broke ranks and fled. Facing death by spear and sword was something they did every day but staring at several hundred fanged jaws of death was too much for even the bravest fighter.

The air filled with the sounds of terrifying feline screeches and the shrieks of men being torn apart. Shango roared his disapproval. Kambon shouted orders to which no one listened.

Mensa laughed.

Shango whirled. "Have you gone mad, Mensa? We are losing the field."

Mensa's face grew serious. "On the contrary, my Lord. We have just won the day."

Shango's face was blank. Mensa continued. "There is more to the Ancient Law – there are consequences for what Ogun has done."

"Explain – quickly."

"There is more to the Law – a second clause – a punishment. The first part says, 'They will not suffer for our evil.' It continues, 'Those who do will endure the wrath of Nature.'"

With chaos enveloping the scene, Shango was in no mood for a philosophy lecture. "How does that help us?"

"Ogun was broken the Law – we now have Nature's blessing to use whatever we need – and the forces of the Earth are on our side."

CHAPTER 26

The Division of Elephants was primarily for show. Comprised of three thousand King Elephants, the largest in Pangea, it was a favorite at every state function and in every parade. Each massive beast stood at least eight cubits[13] tall. No one could guess their weight. With unmatched strength and unsurpassed intelligence, they were the prize of Abzu.

During festivals, each beast was bedecked with a headdress of bright feathers and covered with enough silk to build 300 garments. Bells dangled from their enormous, curved tusks and they swayed back and forth to drum beats and music as if they were dancing. They were so strong, no animal ever challenged one but so gentle that no child ever feared one.

Mensa had anticipated Ogun's deceit – the god could not be trusted, nor did he know all the ancient ways. Without asking permission, Mensa had formed a plan of action just in case Ogun decided to do something heinous.

Using a battalion of men, Mensa gathered thousands of giant palm leaves, which he had sewn together like giant capes. Each "garment" was then tailored to a specific elephant and numbered to avoid confusion. After the cloak had been fitted, Mensa order that each one be covered in resin tapped from the forests – up to fifteen separate coats. When the resin hardened, it formed a thick, almost impenetrable layer like armor. Still, it was light and flexible. Given their gigantic size and im- measurable strength, the beasts would never know they were wearing anything.

They would be almost impervious to harm from spears, swords, and arrows. Mensa might em- ploy the denizens of the forest, but he would honor the sacred order – he would not allow innocent ani- mals to suffer harm.

As soon as he received permission from Kam- bon, Mensa divided the elephants into three com- panies of 750 each. He held the last quarter of the animals in reserve. On his signal, the beasts charged – one company from the right flank, one from the left, and one directly up the middle.

The earth shook as if it would come apart at the seams as the pachyderms rumbled forward. At the first tremor, the leopards stopped their car- nage. They sensed danger. By the third elephantine step, the big cats were in full retreat, rushing past, around, and over their masters – who quickly fol- lowed once they saw the colossal beasts crest the hill.

Shango's troops cheered. Ogun's soldiers fled. The tide of the battle had turned.

Victory was assured.

Until it wasn't.

**

The first blast sounded like a thunderclap. The second looked like a volcanic eruption. Kambon and Mensa flinched when they heard the elephants begin to scream, unearthly, horrific roars of bewilderment and pain. Neither man understood.

But Shango did.

The trio stared in horror as Ogun appeared on the battlefield, black blood trickling from a wound in his shoulder, red blood dripping from the sword in his belt. He had something in his hands – a cylindrical object about three cubits[14] long. Its tip glowed red.

Ogun's face wore a mask of cruel rage. He pointed the cylinder at one of the elephants and pulled back on a lever. There was a blast of white light and the elephant vanished with a terrifying trumpet of pain.

Shango whirled to his companions. Only Kambon remained. Mensa had disappeared.

"What is that, Lord Shango?" Kambon had never shown open fear – anywhere.

"I do not know, General," Shango said. But it was a lie. He had never seen the exact device, but he knew what it was – a portable version of the Worm's technology. It was some form of molecular separator. What they had been using to extract gold from other minerals was not being used to blow living organisms apart. The ray – or pulse – or whatever Ogun had devised – was separating cells from one another and driving the elephants into oblivion.

Apparently it took a while for the "death ray" – or whatever it was – to reload because Ogun waited between each shot. While he could not mow down the elephants like wheat, each and every shot was fatal. Ogun aimed again and another massive beast blew apart.

Kambon was frantic. "Lord Shango, we cannot defeat such a weapon." He paused. "Unless you have one."

Shango's shoulders slumped. "I do not, General. I fear my brother's devious mind will carry the day." He looked around. "Where it that coward, Mensa? Did he desert us?"

Kambon surveyed the field. He broke into a smile. "Hardly, my Lord – Mensa would never abandon Abzu."

Kambon pointed and Shango looked.

Mensa was close to Ogun – close enough to have knocked the weapon from Ogun's hands with a bull whip. Mensa curled the whip again and snapped it. Black blood spurted from Ogun's cheek. Rage filled Ogun's eyes. He stepped from his chariot this time catching the whip as it whistled through the air.

Wrapping the whip around his forearm, he yanked hard. Mensa was strong and brave, but still a mortal. He could not match the god's strength. He flew through the air and landed at Ogun's feet. Ogun unleashed a savage kick followed by an overhand right to the head. Mensa crumpled. Ogun drew his sword and raised it above his head with both hands. This would be a killing blow.

The spear severed the tendon in Ogun's right hand. He howled, dropped the sword, and clutched his bleeding appendage. Hundreds of chariots crested the hill each occupied by a pair of riders – a driver in full battle gear and a second who launched short spears using a leather sling. The "shot" was delivered underhanded and traveled parallel to the ground with blistering speed.

All the occupants of the chariots were women.

Shango shouted in delight. "It is my sister Amma and the women of Tusk," he said. "How did they know to be here."

"It's only a guess, my Lord," Kambon said, "But I think Mensa might have had something to do with it."

Shango looked out over the battlefield. Mensa, still prone on the ground, had his fist raised in triumph.

Epilogue

If this story had begun "Once upon a time," the ending would be different.

Once upon a time, a young man named Mensa won the heart of the Princess he had loved since childhood.

Or...

...Once upon a time, two brothers fought. The younger one, the defender of the human race, won. The elder brother, enraged into conflict by jealousy, recognized his folly, reconciled with his sibling, and changed his ways.

Or...

...Once upon a time, the forces of good overcame the army of evil, turned back an unwarranted attack, and restored peace.

Or...

...Once upon a time, the great god Shango returned to his palace where he and his wife ruled for decades of prosperity and tranquility.

Then, we could add, "and they lived happily ever after."

But this is a legend – not a fairy tale.

**

The battle was over, and the Abzubians trudged home exhausted but triumphant. They carried the bodies of their fallen comrades on stretchers held high above their heads. They told stories of the battle and expressed eagerness to be home – and at peace.

At the front of the procession, Mensa rode with Shango. Their stallions protested the leisurely pace, but it was too hot, and the troops were too tired to force a faster cadence. They would arrive home when they arrived. And they would do so safely.

Ogun and his army had retreated after the formal surrender. Shango watched as Ogun disabled the disintegration machine. Once again, Shango and Amma forced their brother into an agreement he detested but would honor – this time that he would never again employ such technology for any malevolent purpose. As Ogun slumped away with his troops, Amma bade a fond farewell to her victorious brother.

"Peace be with you, Shango," she said.

"And with you and your people, my sister," he said.

"I would love to meet your bride soon," she said. "After all, Ogun is already angry with me, so why should I worry if he becomes upset by my visit to your kingdom."

"You are welcome any time," Shango said. "And you must meet my son."

"Has he a name?"

Shango shook his head. "Not yet. It is the custom of my wife's people to wait until the child is five Earth years. But I have a name in mind."

Amma's eyebrows arched. "You cannot name him for yourself, my brother – that would be unseemly."

"Not at all," Shango said. "But I plan to name him for someone in our line."

"And what name have you chosen?"

Shango displayed a wane smile – one of longing and nostalgia. "I will name him for my brother – the one I never met. I will name the child Marvex."

Amma smiled – Shango could not tell if she knew all this history but decided not to inquire. "It is good," she said. "It is as it should be."

They embraced and Amma left at the head of a column of her fearless female troopers.

Shango and his men neared the city and could see the spires of the palace.

"We are nearly home, Mensa," Shango said. "And it would not have happened without your heroism."

Ever the soldier, Mensa tried to deflect the praise. "I was only doing my duty,
my Lord," he said.

"Somehow I knew you would say that," Shango said. "Still, I have already sent messengers ahead. When we get home, everything will be ready. I intend to honor you with a feast and with something else."

"Nothing is necessary, my Lord," Mensa said.

"For once, soldier, just hold your tongue and listen," Shango said.

When Mensa looked, he saw Shango smiling. "Yes, my Lord," he said.

Shango continued. "We will have a feast – it will last three days as is the custom. At the end of the festivities, I will name you to succeed General Kambon. He has determined it is time to step down."

"My Lord?"

"I appreciate your concern, Mensa. The General retires of his own accord. He realizes his best days as a strategist are behind him. In fact, he recommended you – but I had already made up my mind."

"I am honored, Lord Shango." He hesitated. "What of the Princess?"

Shango laughed. "I knew you would be concerned. You can hand-pick her bodyguards – and you can see her whenever you wish. I realize now how foolishly wrong I was about you. Even someone as thick-headed and vain as I am would never keep a man from seeing his 'sister.'"

"Thank you, my Lord."

They rode in silence for a while. Shango's head snapped up when Mensa finally spoke again. "My Lord, look."

It was the palace bestrewn with festive banners and flags of all colors.

"They are ready to welcome the conquering hero, my Lord," Mensa said.

"I imagine they are," Shango said. "I told them you were coming."

Both men laughed and rode towards their mutual triumph.

They drew close enough to see figures on the balcony.

"That is the window outside my bedroom," Shango said. "Look there. It is Nefertari."

The Princess stood on the balcony waving a brightly-color pennant. Three of her attendants stood by her side, each with a banner of a different color.

Shango and Mensa both beamed but their expressions turned to ones of horror in the next second.

Fire and smoke billowed from the balcony. Moments later, a booming noise and concussive blast spooked the horses. The men held on but only through superior mounted skill.

When the smoke cleared, nothing remained of the balcony.

And Nefertari was nowhere to be seen.

---

[1] A cubit = distance from a man's elbow to the tip of his middle finger/approximately 18 inches – Dindaka is about 6'4"

[2] Seven-and-a-half feet

[3] 3 feet

[4] 45 feet

[5] 3 feet

[6] 7.5 feet

[7] 12 feet

[8] 30 feet

Balewa A Sample

[9] 9.75 feet

[10] Each year in Nauru = approximately 45 years on Earth

[11] What Earth scientists Watson and Crick eventually labeled "DNA"

[12] 1 furlong = ~1/8th of a mile

[13] 8 cubits = 12 feet

[14] 3 cubits = 4.5 feet

Made in the USA
Monee, IL
23 November 2019